Bread and Roses, Too

KATHERINE PATERSON

sandpiper

Houghton Mifflin Harcourt
Boston New York

The text was set in Berkeley Book.

www.hmhco.com

Library of Congress Cataloging-in-Publication Data

Paterson, Katherine.
Bread and roses, too / by Katherine Paterson
p. cm.
Summary: Jake and Rosa, two children, form an unlikely
friendship as they try to survive and understand the 1912 Bread and Roses
strike of mill workers in Lawrence, Massachusetts.
HC ISBN-13: 978-0-618-65479-6
PA ISBN-13: 978-0-547-07651-5
[1. Strikes and lockouts—Textile workers—Fiction. 2. Labor unions
—Fiction. 3. Survival—Fiction. 4. Textile workers—Fiction.
5. Immigrants—Fiction. 6. Emigration and immigration—Fiction.
7. Lawrence (Mass.)—History—20th century—Fiction.] I. Title.
PZ7.P273Bq   2006
[Fic] — dc22   2005031702

Printed in the U.S.A.
DOC   10 9 8
4500633464

Bread and Roses, Too

For Karen Lane, Barre's extraordinary librarian,
with gratitude and affection

and in memory of Vermont's premier labor
historian, Dr. Richard Hathaway

and in honor of all those in our society who,
despite their labor, receive less than a living wage

"This was more than a union. It was a crusade for a united people—for 'Bread and Roses.'"

—Elizabeth Gurley Flynn
The Rebel Girl: An Autobiography

❧ Contents ❧

Bread and Roses, Too

One

Shoe Girl

THE TENEMENTS LOOMED toward the sky on either side of the alley like glowering giants, but they'd keep the wind off. There was plenty of trash in the narrow space between them. It stank to high heaven, but, then, so did he. He began to burrow into the heap like a rat. A number of rodents squawked and scrambled away. *Hell's bells!* He hoped they wouldn't bite him while he was asleep. Rat bites hurt like fury. For a moment he stopped digging, but the freezing air drove him farther in. He tried to warm himself by cursing his pa. The words inside his head were hot as flaming hades, but they didn't fool his hands and feet, which ached from the cold.

He'd heard of people freezing to death in their sleep. It happened to drunks all the time. He sometimes wished it would happen to his pa, although he knew it was wicked to wish your own pa dead. But how could Jake be expected to care whether the brute lived or died? The man did nothing but beat him. *Dead, he wouldn't beat me*

1

or steal all my pay for drink—and then beat me for not earning more.

He was keeping himself agitated, if not warm, with hateful thoughts of the old man when he heard light footsteps close by. He willed himself motionless.

It was a small person from the sound, and coming right for his pile. *You can't have my pile. This one's mine. I already claimed it. I chased the rats for it. I made my nest in it. . . .* He began to growl.

"Who's there?" It was the frightened voice of a child—a girl, if he wasn't mistaken.

"What do you want?" He stuck his head out of the pile.

The girl jumped back with a little shriek.

Stupid little mouse.

"Who are you?" she asked, her voice shaking.

"It's my pile. Go away."

"I don't want your pile. Really, I don't." She was shaking so hard, her whole body was quivering. "I—I just need to look in it—to find something."

"In here?"

"I think so. I'm not sure."

He was interested in spite of himself. "What did you lose?"

"My—my shoes," she said.

"How could you lose your shoes?"

"I guess I sort of hid them."

"You *what?*"

"I know," she said. He could tell she was about to bawl. "It was stupid. I really need new ones. But Mamma said Anna had to stand up all day on the line and she needed shoes worse than me. I thought if I lost mine . . . It was stupid, I know." She began to cry in earnest.

"Okay, okay, which pile?" He stood up, old bottles, cans, and papers cascading from his shoulders.

She put her left foot on top of her right, to keep at least one stockinged foot from touching the frozen ground. "You smell awful," she said.

"Shut up. You want help or not?"

"Please," she said. "I'm sorry."

They dug about in the dark. At length, Jake found the first shoe, and then the girl found the other. She nodded gratefully, slipped them on her feet, and bent over to tie what was left of the laces.

"You didn't lose them so good."

"No. I guess I knew all along I'd have to find them." She gave a little sigh. "But thank you." She was very polite. He figured she went to school even in shoes that were more holes than leather. "You can't sleep in a garbage heap," she said.

"And why not?"

"You'll freeze to death is why." Somehow with her shoes found, she didn't seem like a scared mouse after all.

"I done it before. Besides, where else am I gonna go?"

"You might—you can sleep in our kitchen." She blurted the words out, and then put her hand quickly to her mouth.

"Your folks might notice," he said. "Besides I stink. You said so."

"We all stink." She grabbed his arm. "Come on before I change my mind."

They went in the alley door of one of the buildings and climbed to the third floor. "Shh," she said before she opened the door. "They're all asleep."

She led him between the beds in the first room and then into the kitchen. There was no fire in the stove, but the room was warmer than a trash pile.

"You can lie down here," she said. "We don't have an extra bed—not even a quilt. I'm sorry."

"I'll be okay," he said. He could hardly make out her features in the dark room, but he could tell that she was smaller than he and very thin, with hair that hung to her shoulders.

"I'll be up before your pa wakes," he said.

"He's dead. Nobody will throw you out."

Still, the first stirring in the back room woke him the next morning. A kid was crying out and a woman's voice was trying to shush it, though Jake reckoned it to be a hunger cry that could not be hushed with words.

He got silently to his feet. There was a box on the

table. He opened it to find a half loaf of bread. He tore off a chunk, telling himself they'd never miss it. Then he stole back through the front room, where someone was snoring like thunder, and out the door and down the stairs and on down the hill to the mill and to work. No danger of freezing there. He never stopped moving. Why, even on these frigid winter mornings, he was sweating like a pig by ten o'clock.

Later he remembered that he hadn't even asked the girl her name or told her his.

Two

"Short Pay! All Out!"

"SHORT PAY!" It was one of the Italians. Halfway back in the line waiting for his pay envelope, Jake felt a thrill of fear or excitement, he couldn't have said which. All week the men had talked of a strike. The Italians had passed around a petition. If you signed it, you were promising to walk out if the threatened pay cut came through in Friday's envelope. None of the Irish, who were mostly management or skilled, nor any of the other native-born, had signed it. But Jake had put his X on it, mostly because his pa had threatened to kill him if he went out on strike "with those wops," and Jake, as usual, had been furious with him. The sot had drunk up all of Jake's last pay envelope so that he had had to spend the past two weeks stealing food and sleeping in garbage dumps just to stay alive.

At first the non-Italian workers seemed confused. Should they walk out or stay put? Several started back toward their stations, then changed their minds and

6

followed the Italians. Paddy Parker, the Irish floor boss, had planted himself at the head of the escalator, trying to block anyone's attempted exit with his huge body. Billy Wood, owner of half the mills in town, was uncommonly proud of that escalator. It got the workers from the ground floor to the upper stories of the mill in record time. That, with the speeded-up machines, was swelling the profit margin at the Wood Mill.

"Strike! Strike!" another worker cried, racing back and forth between the rows of spindle frames. Someone pulled a switch, and the belts slowed and stopped.

"Strike! Strike!" And then, pandemonium. Jake heard his own voice join the roar. "Short pay! All out!" He heard the sound of wood shattering and saw knives slashing across the great belts. He grabbed a fire bucket and threw the filthy water on the gleaming white thread. The smell of wet wool filled his nostrils. He took the empty bucket and heaved it against the line of spindles, breaking three of them. The power of it filled him like cheap wine. He smashed three more, then another two before someone—Angelo Corti, as it turned out— grabbed him by the back of his shirt. "Come on, boy, everyone's getting out!"

Jake bashed another three or four spindles before dropping the bucket. The big man's hand still held tight to his shirt. He tried to shake it away, but Angelo yanked him the length of the floor, past Paddy Parker, and down the nonworking escalator. Someone had obviously broken Mr. Wood's pride and joy, or at least shut it off.

The iron gates to the mill yard were locked—it was only eleven forty-five in the morning—but several large Italians found the gatekeeper and persuaded him, none too gently, to unlock it.

"Short pay! All out!"

It was spitting snow. Jake had no jacket, and his thin cotton pants and shirt were no protection against the wind. Once outside the gates, he planned to hightail it east for the shelter of his shack near the river. He could have easily weaseled his way through the chanting mob. Angelo had let go his shirt the moment they passed the big front doors, but he couldn't make himself leave.

"Short pay! All out! Short pay! All out!"

He crossed the bridge as though hypnotized and allowed himself to be carried by the mob from the Wood to the other mills—to the Ayer, the Washington, and on to the Atlantic and the three Pacific mills—gathering men and women and children strikers at each place. The city riot bells had commenced a frenzied clanging, and whistles screamed at them from the top of every mill as they passed. The workers chanted louder to drown out the panicked alarms of the authorities.

As storm winds gather power, so did the mass of strikers. There must have been hundreds of them—no, thousands—all chanting, "Short pay! All out!" And the workers were pouring out of the mills as they passed each gate. Not only the Italians but all those strange people from other parts of the world—Poles and Lithuanians and Russians and Syrians and Jews and Greeks and Portuguese and Armenians and countries and languages he'd never heard of, taking up the cry, in maybe the only words of English they knew: "Short pay! All out!"

He patted his pocket. His pay envelope was still there—less twenty-five cents, the cost of a week of beer for himself. But enough to pay the rent on the shack and buy him food for the next two weeks if he could keep it away from his pa. Or he could just give the old man half and tell him that short pay meant half of what he got last payday. Maybe on the way home he should stop by and buy a bottle. If the old man had a few swigs, he might believe the lie.

Pa would be raging mad about the strike. Best not to tell him he'd joined up. It couldn't last long—probably be over by Monday or so. Nobody could afford to stay out long in the wintertime. They'd freeze before they starved.

"How you feeling, Jake?" It was Angelo, slapping him on the back, treating him like a man, something his own father never did.

"Swell," he said, joining the chant again: "Short pay! All out!" Kids were hanging out the schoolhouse windows staring at him—envying him, he reckoned. He stood up straighter and chanted louder.

When the marchers got to the Plains neighborhood, where most of the workers lived in mill-owned tenements, they began to separate. Some of the men were talking of forming a picket line around the mills to keep scabs from returning after the dinner hour. Others were talking about strike meetings that night to plan strategy, but Jake could catch only the English words dropped into the foreigners' talk—words like "scab" and "strike." Angelo turned to him. "I guess you native-born got no strike organization," he said, a big smile on his face.

Jake shook his head. He had yet to see a regular American or an Irishman in the crowd.

"You wanna join us Italians tonight? Be a good meeting, I promise you."

"Yeah, sure," Jake said. Anything to postpone the strapping he was sure to get when he went home.

"Meantime," said Angelo. "I got money in my pocket. How about some grub? My treat."

The tavern was full of Italians spraying tomato sauce as they jabbered excitedly at each other. Angelo told Jake to sit down, and then he disappeared across the crowded, smoky room. Soon he returned, bringing two huge platters of spaghetti to the table. He set one of them in front of Jake. It was the most beautiful sight he had ever seen. The tomato sauce even sported a few bits of greasy sausage. Jake forgot the crowd around him, forgot the strike, forgot the menace that waited for him in the shack, and fell to, his nose almost in the steaming plate. He hadn't had a full platter of food to himself in his entire thirteen years of life.

"Hey, hey, take a breath, boy. Enjoy!" Angelo said, plunking down a glass of red wine in front of Jake. He sat down on the bench next to him, but before long he was jawing with his pals—eating and drinking at the same time—just like everyone around them.

The talk was all in Italian. Jake knew only a few words; most of them he suspected were cusses, because he often heard them muttered behind Paddy Parker's back. Then, seemingly without warning, the men around him jumped to their feet.

"We're going down to picket, Jake boy," Angelo said. "Try to keep the blasted scabs from coming back in after the noon hour. You wanna come?"

Jake shrugged. It was the end of free food and drink, so he might as well join them. It was better than the leather strap waiting for him at the shack. He grabbed his glass and drained the last few warming drops.

They marched down Union Street in a body, chanting, "Short pay! All out!" and blocking the street entirely so that no one, much less a wagon or buggy or auto, could get past. When the mills lining Canal Street came in view, the roar grew louder. It wasn't just men and boys—there were women and girls as well, maybe more of them than men. The women were smiling and laughing, as though heading out on a gigantic picnic. Some of the crowd stopped to surround the gate at the Everett, others broke off at Canal to cut off entry into the Washington, the Atlantic, and the Pacific mills. Jake followed Angelo toward the bridge across the Merrimack, back to the Wood Mill, which they'd left less than an hour earlier.

"Scab! Scab!" they yelled at anyone trying to muscle his or her way through their midst. "Make a line! Make a line!" someone shouted. Angelo grabbed Jake's arm, and then, grasping hands, the crowd of marchers spread out in a line that kept anyone from crossing the bridge and entering the gates of the Wood.

Jake was watching Angelo, so when the icy water came gushing down on his head, he looked up to see if it could be pouring rain in the middle of January.

"Fire hoses!" Angelo yelled. "They're setting the blasted fire hoses on us!"

Some of the women and girls screamed. They were all soaked through before they could get out of range of the hoses. A few hardy souls, including Angelo, started for the bridge. Jake ran to catch up with him, but then a stream of water hit him in the chest and knocked him flat on his back.

"It's no good!" Angelo yelled over the racket of water and human cries, grabbing Jake's hand and pulling him to his feet. "They break our bones and freeze us to death if we stay. Go home," he said to the departing backs of the workers, and almost to himself. "Yes, go home, it's all right." Then he shouted, though no one on the other side of the bridge could have heard him over the sound made by the torrents of water, "We be back! You see, Mr. Billy Wood. We don't give up!"

It seemed to Jake, shivering in the freezing gray afternoon, that they *had* given up. They'd all run as soon as the water hit them. Not that he had stayed. He wasn't a fool.

"You got more clothes, Jake boy?"

Jake shook his head. "It don't matter."

"You got fire at home?"

"Naw, it don't matter."

"You come to Angelo's and get warm. Can't have you sick. We got too much to do now."

❧ Three

The Best Student

Rosa was sitting quietly at her desk, her eyes on her history book, when the riot bells began to ring. All the children were suddenly roused out of sleep or stupor. The bells did not sound like any they had ever heard; it was as though madmen had been let loose in the city hall tower.

Rosa looked at her teacher, Miss Finch, who was sitting perfectly erect at her desk, her eyes wide like those of an animal who has been startled and is too frightened to flee. Rosa watched as the teacher slowly rose to her feet and walked over to the window. It was grimy and the sill sooty, so she was careful not to touch anything. Then she left the window and came back to the space behind her desk. The shrill blasts of factory whistles pierced through the clang of the city hall bells. Some of the children covered their ears against the racket, but Miss Finch gave a little shake of her head, as though to dismiss both the bells and the whistles.

"Yes. Where were we?" She glanced down at her book. "All right. Who knows who Thomas Jefferson was?"

Only Rosa raised her hand. She raised it up barely halfway, glancing around at her classmates as she did so. Most of their heads were still cocked, as they listened to the strange shrieking and clanging that went on and on. She was instantly ashamed for them—their faces gray with the grime that never seemed to scrub off. Marco Bartolini's nose was running, as usual. When he caught her looking, he dropped his eyes and rubbed his nose across his ragged sleeve. She looked away hastily.

"Hasn't anyone besides Rosa read the assignment?" Miss Finch sighed to indicate how her pupils constantly disappointed her. "All right, Rosa. Tell the others what you know about Thomas Jefferson."

How much should Rosa say? Besides the pages in the textbook, she had read a whole library book about the third president. In the silence, the insistent bells seemed to crash even more threateningly.

"We're waiting, Rosa."

"He—he was the third president of the United States."

"Yes. But before that. What did he author that was important to history?"

The children turned from staring at the window to look at Rosa. She hated to be the only one to answer Miss Finch's questions. But she had to hurry. The bells demanded it.

"The—the—the—"

"No need to stutter, Rosa." The teacher was actually tapping her foot in time with the bells.

"The—the—the Declaration of Independence."

"Very good, Rosa." The teacher turned to the rest of the class. "All the information you need to know about Thomas Jefferson is in the textbook that each of you *should* have read last night."

No! No! No! The bells accused them. *Help! Help! Help!* The whistles screamed.

"Marco, did you read your assignment?"

He hung his head. With the single exception of Joe O'Brien, everyone, including Rosa, did the same. They knew what was coming next.

"Do you even *own* a textbook, Marco? Brigid? Tony? Pierre? Luigi? Marta?" Each child in turn gave a shake of his or her head, never meeting the teacher's stern gaze.

"Is Rosa Serutti the only person in this class whose parents have realized the importance of buying a history textbook? How many times do I have to repeat myself? It is useless to come to school if your parents do not provide you with textbooks. You need to speak to them about the importance of education. How many of your parents are enrolled in the evening classes?"

No one raised a hand. How could their parents work long hours in the mill and then go to school at night? They were tired all the time as it was. The children—all but Joe O'Brien—sagged into their rigid seats, their heads so low that their chins nearly scraped the splintery desktops. It didn't matter that they'd heard this, or similar lectures, from Miss Finch since September. It still stung as bitterly as the January wind rattling the window of the schoolroom while the tower bell clanged, *Dunce! Dunce! Dunce!*

The Khoury brothers had fallen asleep as usual, despite the bells, which eventually stopped, only to be replaced by a shrillness in Miss Finch's usually quiet voice.

"You must go home today and urge your parents not to strike." The lace jabot at her throat bobbed up and down. Rosa watched her, fascinated.

"Do you understand, boys and girls?" The teacher's voice went up several more notes. "I know Mr. Wood personally. A kinder, more compassionate employer you couldn't hope to find. He wants what is best for his workers, believe me. Tell your parents that he was a mill operative himself long ago. Did you know that?"

All the children snapped to attention. The big boss of the American Woolen Company once worked in the mills?

"Yes, not everyone knows this. He started in the mills as a boy, but through hard work and *education* he rose to be the owner of many mills. Do you see what education means, children? Without an education, you'll lose any chance of a life better than the one your parents know."

"I thought, ma'am," said Joe O'Brien, who was both

saucy and Irish, "I thought Billy Wood got to be the owner because he married his boss's daughter."

Miss Finch's pale face colored slightly. "Yes, Joseph, that's true. But if Mr. Wood hadn't bettered himself through hard work and education, that never could have happened."

Everyone knew that Mr. Billy Wood had a huge estate in Andover and more cars than he himself could count. Rosa thought a small, clean house with room for a garden would be enough. She didn't want a car. She was afraid of cars. They were fast and reckless and made of cold, unfeeling metal. Mrs. Marino's husband had been killed by one. Mrs. Marino was Mamma's friend and lived just across the alley, and she told the story of her husband's death over and over again, adding more terrifying details each time. A horse and buggy would be nice. But Miss Finch was right. She must get her education or she'd end up in the mills like her big sister, Anna.

Anna didn't care about education the way Rosa did. Rosa was sure of that. When Papa died after the mill fire, the first thing Anna had said to Mamma was: "I'll quit school and go to work." Mamma had tried to protest, saying that Anna wouldn't be fourteen for almost two more years, but what could she do? Without Papa's eight dollars and seventy-five cents a week, there was no way they could live on Mamma's six dollars and twenty-five cents—especially with the new baby coming. So Mamma had paid the man who fixed papers to change Anna's age, and Anna had gone to work. But they still couldn't live on what she and Mamma made together, so Mamma had taken in the Lithuanian family. That wouldn't have been so bad if Granny Jarusalis hadn't snored. Rosa liked Granny, but she hated sleeping with an old Lithuanian woman who snored.

"Some of you children are not listening," Miss Finch was saying. "Don't you understand that the bell you heard earlier was the city riot bell? I'm sure your parents don't want a city under mob rule, but if they listen to the rabble-rousers and go out on strike, that may well happen. And I'm terribly afraid that you children will be the ones who suffer."

Rosa forced herself to keep her head up and listen to the teacher. It was hard to pay attention, especially since breakfast had been only dry bread with a smear of molasses. Granny Jarusalis might give her cabbage soup for dinner, if the old woman could borrow a cabbage leaf or two from one of her friends. Oh, how Rosa longed for Mamma's rigatoni with tomato sauce seasoned with a bit of meat or even the cheese ravioli that Mrs. Marino used to swap on Sundays for some of the rigatoni. Their balconies were so close that Mamma would just lean over and hand her dish to Mrs. Marino, and Mrs. Marino would hand hers back. Sometimes people walking in the alley three floors down would smell the food and look up. "Don'ta worry!" Mrs. Marino would yell. "We don'ta drop on your stupid head. Too precious!"

But there hadn't been any precious rigatoni or ravioli to share for many Sundays now. They'd hardly been able to afford even plain, boiled macaroni since Papa died. If Mamma and Anna went out on strike, there wouldn't be money for bread and molasses. Rosa felt better when she realized that. Mamma wouldn't be so foolish. She loved Anna and Rosa and little Ricci too much to go out on strike.

Rosa came to with a start. She had been daydreaming, blocking out the teacher's words. "I'm sure that you boys and girls, who have studied arithmetic, realize that no one could afford to pay the same wages for less work. You'd lose money—"

"Hear that?" yelled Joe O'Brien right in the middle of Miss Finch's lecture. He ran to the window. Most of the class followed him over, leaving only the Khoury brothers and Rosa at their desks.

"Sit down!" Miss Finch commanded, but no one except Rosa was listening. Joe threw up the window, and a cold blast of wind carried the sounds of shouts and chanting into the schoolroom. At first it was a blur, but then Rosa could make out the words: "Short pay! All out! Short pay! All out!!" over and over again. She now got up and made her way across the room, leaving only the still sleeping Khoury boys at their desks.

She pushed her way to the window and looked down. The crowd marching below seemed immense. She could almost feel the heat of their anger as they shouted in unison. "Short pay! All out!"

Behind the children, Miss Finch fluttered and begged and commanded, but none of them left the window. The bell had warned, but now they knew that in that crowd their world was turning upside-down. "There's my mamma!" Celina Cosa cried. She leaned over the sill and waved. "Mamma! Mamma! *Guarda qui!* Up here!" as though someone from below could have heard a child's voice over the chants of thousands, as the stream of marchers coming up from the mills on the river seemed unending.

"Sit down!" Miss Finch's face was red and blotched, her eyes wide, like a frightened horse.

No one sat down for the length of time it took the line of marchers to pass under the window and around the corner of the street, leaving behind the sound of their defiance. "Short pay! All out!"

Not long after the children had reluctantly returned to their seats, the bell rang. They looked now to their teacher for the words of dismissal that would send them out to an hour of freedom, since dinner hour promised very little dinner in any of the tenements these days.

Miss Finch, still red-faced, acted almost as though she had not heard the bell. The children shifted restlessly in their seats. At last, she sighed, looking at them with such disappointment in her eyes that all except Joe O'Brien hung their heads again. "I am not sure it is safe to let you out on the streets." She shuddered. "There is no telling what an angry mob will do. Why, you might be trampled to death—the mood that mob is in!"

They sat there, staring at their desktops, some of them, no doubt, more willing to risk trampling by their loving parents in the streets than to remain imprisoned with their teacher indefinitely. They sat tense and silent, eyes on desks, ears straining in vain to hear the chanting of the strikers. Finally, Miss Finch shook her head. "Dismissed," she said, in the tone of one resigning another to certain ruin.

The children jumped to their feet and jostled each other to get out the door, all but the still sleeping brothers and Rosa. Rosa got her history book—the only one Mamma had been able to afford—out of her desk and started slowly for the door.

"Rosa."

She turned at the sound of her name. Miss Finch was sitting at her desk, straightening books and papers.

"Yes, Miss Finch."

"I have hopes for you, Rosa. You're not like the others. You're bright and ambitious. Don't let anyone lead you astray."

"No, ma'am."

"No matter what your father says. You must stay in school. You understand?"

"He's dead, ma'am," Rosa whispered.

"Sorry?"

"Papa's dead."

"Oh, I'm sorry. I should have known that." She fumbled a bit with some pencils. "But it doesn't change what I'm saying. You mustn't let your mother—"

"No, ma'am."

She guessed Miss Finch would like her to say that her mother stayed home like a proper American lady and took care of the family. Ever since she had been in the first grade, all her teachers had told the children that in proper homes, unlike the foreign tenements in the Plains, men went out to work and supported their families and women stayed home and cooked nutritious meals and took care of their children. This was the ideal they were to aim for—to leave behind the unnatural lives of their immigrant parents and become Americans. What Miss Finch didn't explain was why American women needed to go to school and study hard if they were just going to stay home and have babies, or why she, with an education, had no husband or babies. It was all very confusing. Still, the one thing that Rosa had learned in her nearly six years of schooling was that education was the key to escape from the mills. If that meant listening to her teachers rail against the ignorance and filth of home

23

life in the Plains, then she must put up with it. Although she couldn't help the anger that welled up inside her whenever teachers acted as though her mamma were ignorant and uncaring, just because her English was broken and she couldn't afford to buy Rosa clothes, much less books. Rosa could hardly blame them. How could someone like Miss Finch, in her perfectly laundered and pressed clothes, with her soft white hands, and smooth unwrinkled face, know how wise and loving and truly beautiful her mamma was?

"And Rosa—"

"Yes, Miss Finch?"

"Wake up the Khoury boys before you go, please."

She was late already and, with the crowds of workers in the streets, liable to be even later getting home for her meager lunch, but she did as the teacher asked. She shook each of the brothers gently until they sleepily stumbled to their feet. She felt no further obligation, so she rushed out the door and ran down the stairs. She had long outgrown her only jacket, and the January wind off the river pierced her thin cotton dress and stabbed her bones. Maybe Granny J. would let her borrow her shawl tomorrow. She must ask secretly. Mamma would never permit it—taking the warmth from an old woman's shoulders. But it was so cold. And Granny could use one of the bed quilts for a shawl, couldn't she?

The street was crowded with people, all excited, all

jabbering in as many languages as the city knew. It was hard to force her way through the mass, and she felt a little desperate. She didn't want to get caught up in a mob. Even if one part of her knew that the crowd was made up of neighbors and friends—people like her own family—another part had been chilled by Miss Finch's warnings. Although her head told her that Mamma would never risk starving her children, something in her stomach made her search the angry, excited faces as she pushed through the milling crowds on the street, half afraid that she would see her mother's face.

She was panting when she got to the third-floor apartment and pushed open the door. The Jarusalis boys were squabbling in the bedroom. In the kitchen, little Ricci was crying, as he too often was, and Granny J. was sitting in a chair, rocking back and forth and saying mysterious cooing words in her own strange language, trying to comfort him. He was so tiny. Who could believe he was more than a year old?

"Noise!" Granny J. said, looking up from the squalling child on her lap. "Noise! Too big."

Rosa nodded. "Is Mamma here? Anna?"

Granny J. shook her head. The gray and white hairs didn't cover her old pinkish scalp. "Nobody. I make soup good. Nobody come."

The words were hardly out before the door burst open: Mrs. J. and her daughter, Marija, with Mamma and

Anna close behind. Of course, it was their mealtime, too. They'd only just gotten here—what with all the crowds—

"We walked out!" Anna's eyes were shining. "We simply walked out. Everyone! We're out on strike!"

Four

For the Needy

Hᴏᴡ ᴄᴏᴜʟᴅ Rᴏsᴀ go back to school? Everything was in chaos in the streets. When Mamma and Anna had joined the strikers at the mill gate, they had been doused with water from the fire hoses. Now Mamma was lying in bed shivering, even though Rosa had put every quilt in the flat on top of her. And as hard as Rosa pleaded for her to stay home, Anna was determined to go out somewhere to consult with all the other lawbreakers, acting as though a strike was the most wonderful thing that had ever happened in her life. Mrs. Jarusalis and Marija had already left. Apparently, the Lithuanians were meeting in one place, and the Italians in another.

"Tell Anna not to go, Mamma. Please."

But Mamma refused to stop her. "She goes with Mrs. Marino."

"But Mrs. Marino has a hot temper. You know that, Mamma."

Mamma gave a laugh that turned into a cough. "I go,

too—soon as I stop the shaking and the barking," she said.

"Please, Mamma, you and Anna mustn't strike. You might get hurt. The mobs will get violent." She couldn't say what she was really thinking. *What will we eat? How will we pay the rent?*

"Rosa, you understand? They short the pay two hours every week. That is five loaf of bread we don' have no more. I work . . . my children starve. I go out to strike . . . my children starve. Whatever I do, we starve. Is better to fight and starve than work and starve, yes?"

Rosa struggled to make a better argument—anything to keep her mamma and sister safe—but Ricci was crying and she couldn't think straight.

"Now, go help Granny with Ricci. Be some use, smart schoolgirl. I got to be there tomorrow to meet Mr. Joe Ettor. He's going to help us win."

Who was Joe Ettor? To hear Mamma tell, he was a coming savior, but Rosa could only suppose that he was one of the rabble-rousers whom Miss Finch warned about. Someone who might provoke the strikers to violence. *Hail Mary, full of grace, don't let this union thug come and destroy us.*

Angelo lived in a fourth-floor apartment in one of the tenements on Elm Street in the Plains with four other Italian men—all mill workers, it seemed. Angelo handed

Jake a large shirt and told him to take off his wet clothes. The talk in the apartment as the men changed their clothes was as lively as the talk in the tavern before the soaking. One of the men had lit a fire in their small coal stove. The fumes soon filled the kitchen, making Jake's eyes water and his head ache. He began to cough, nearly falling off the chair on which he was sitting.

Angelo yelled something, and one of the men in the back room opened a door out onto the balcony, which helped clear the air and made breathing a bit easier. Jake tucked his bare legs and feet up under Angelo's heavy shirt. Angelo handed him an oversized cup of very hot, very black coffee. Jake warmed his hands on the thick porcelain and occasionally took a sip, slurping air to keep the scalding liquid from burning his throat.

The longer he sat, the sleepier he became—the warm room, the dry shirt, the boisterous clamor of the men gradually fading to a rippling murmur—Angelo must have added a slug of spirits to the coffee. That must be it. His head began to nod. With a leap, Angelo took the cup from his hands, put it on the table, and then carried him to a bed that felt like a cloud beneath his exhausted body.

When Angelo woke him, the room was already dark, though it must have been only late afternoon. He could smell food cooking on the coal stove. "Wake up, sleepy.

We gotta eat and get to our meeting. You wanna come?" Angelo grinned. "Nobody but wops."

"Is my shirt and britches dry?" Jake hated the thought of leaving this warm bed and taking off Angelo's wonderful shirt that covered him nearly to his ankles.

Angelo checked the clothesline over the stove. "Wet as a *bambino's* bottom," he reported. "But Giuliano is short like a girl. We borrow his shirt and britches for tonight, yes?" The one named Giuliano seemed to protest, but it was in Italian, so Jake didn't know if it was because of being compared to a girl or having his clothes appropriated.

They ate their supper of beans and bread, grumbling that it wasn't spaghetti. Jake finished his so quickly that Angelo gave him a second helping. He mopped up the last of the juice with the bread—the crusty bread was wonderful—and longed for a third helping, but the pot was empty and the men were getting up, signaling, alas, that the meal was done.

He couldn't go home, not in Giuliano's clothes, so he went with them to Chabis Hall. He'd seen the plain frame building from the outside many times, but no one who wasn't Italian ever went in there. The hall was dimly lit and crowded. Many were smoking cheap cigars and cigarettes, which fouled the air more than Angelo's coal stove, but somehow the electricity in the room made up for everything. It wasn't the excitement Jake felt when he stole food from the grocer's and got chased down the street. That was thrilling, of course, since he always managed to outrun his pursuer. This was the excitement of being a thief in the middle of hundreds of thieves, all set to steal away the world of Mr. Billy Wood, with his mansion in Andover and more automobiles than even the blooming millionaire himself could count.

That the talk was all in Italian was frustrating, but when the crowd quieted and began to listen to individual speakers, Angelo whispered a few words in English to Jake, so he could get an idea of what was being said.

"Mr. Billy Wood don't understand when we speak soft, speak reason, tell him we are cold and hungry while he is fat and rich. So now we speak strike. That is language he will understand when he have no more profit."

"Shh." A man, sitting in the row ahead, had turned around. He whispered something fierce in Italian, which made Angelo put his arm protectively around Jake's shoulders.

"Joe Ettor say we are all Americans," he said. The man shrugged.

"Who's Joe Ettor?" Jake couldn't help asking.

"Come tomorrow night," Angelo said. "Then you see."

Jake was beginning to believe that the meeting would go on forever when the men around him stood up and cheered and then began to talk noisily among themselves. Still jabbering, the crowd streamed out into the dark street. "Come on, Jake," Angelo said. "Time to celebrate our big strike."

Soon, however, Angelo was so wrapped up in strike talk that he seemed to forget that Jake couldn't understand the blinking Italian gabble. He followed them to a tavern. Although there wasn't a single light burning, one of the Italians grabbed the door handle and yanked. It was locked. The second tavern was dark as well, but there was a crudely lettered sign on the door. "What it say, Angelo?" someone yelled.

The crowd parted to let Angelo get to the door. He bent close to the sign. "It say—" he said, reading the English words—"it say, 'CLOSED BY ORDER OF THE POLICE.'"

The men began to curse in language even Jake could understand. "The blasted police close down the taverns because we strike," Angelo said. "Come on, we go to Marco's. He always got home-made."

But something held Jake back. He knew it was harder for Angelo and his friends to have him hanging on. He'd have to face his father sooner or later. So somewhere along the dark street, he slipped away from his noisy companions and headed down the hill.

He was still wearing Giuliano's clothes, the waist tied with a string to keep the pants from falling down, as he made his way through the cold darkness of the night

back to the shack. Pa was waiting for him, pacing the dirt
floor, spitting out curses against the world in general and
Jake in particular. Too late Jake remembered that he'd
meant to buy a bottle for Pa. He tried to run as soon as
he saw how furious the man was, but it was cold and he
was tired and Pa was too quick for him.

He snatched Jake by the arm and held on like the
devil himself, his long nails biting into Jake's flesh.
"Where you been, you thieving bastard?"

Jake knew better than to answer such a question.

His pa pulled him close, his stinking breath in Jake's
face. In the smoky light of the oil lamp, the man squinted
at Jake's clothes. "Wop clothes!" he declared. "You been
with those damn strikers, ain't you? Take 'em off!"

Jake hesitated just long enough for the man to smack
him across the face. Then he untied the string and
dropped his pants.

"Shirt, too."

Jake obeyed.

With a practiced motion, his father undid his belt
and began to lash Jake's legs and then his back. The boy
bit his lip to keep from screaming out. Finally, Pa's arm
tired, and he dropped the belt to the dirt floor.

Holding Jake fast, Pa picked up Giuliano's pants and
felt the pockets until he found the pay envelope, still
soggy from the earlier soaking. "Ha!" he said. In his
greed, he let go of Jake's arm to pull out the envelope,

and Jake took the chance to jump away from his reach. He grabbed the shirt and pants and started running. He never stopped until he was in the shade of the giant mill, where he dressed himself once more, tears of anger stinging his cheeks.

The boy was too ashamed to go back to Angelo's, so he headed for a place he knew was never locked up—the Irish church, Saint Mary's, on Haverhill Street.

He made his way through the dark sanctuary—the only light, the pale one above the altar—into the room to the left of the altar where the priests kept their robes. He knew from past experience that there was a toilet there and a basin. He fumbled his way in the dark until he found the basin. Standing before it, he stripped himself of Giuliano's clothes, now soggy with his blood. He turned on the water and, with the towel that was hanging next to the basin, washed the bloody stripes on his legs. They stung like fury. He swiped the towel across his back.

Should he try to rinse the blood off Giuliano's clothes? And wear what? A priest's robe? He laughed out loud. He, Jake Beale, got up like a papist priest! In his father's eyes, that would be the only thing worse than a wop's shirt and trousers. So there in the dark, in the priests' private basin, he washed the blood from Giuliano's shirt and pants as best he could and hung them over the heavy chairs in the priests' room to dry.

Then he opened the closet and found himself a nice wool robe with a sash and wrapped himself in it. It was warmer than Angelo's shirt had been.

His eyes had grown accustomed to the dark room, so he investigated the cabinets, where he found a carafe of wine and funny little pieces of dry crackers. He stuffed handfuls of the round crackers into his mouth and washed them down with the wine. It was sweet and tasted a lot better than the wine Angelo had given him in the tavern. He sat down on the soft carpet and drank more of it until the pain in his back and legs dimmed and his head began to nod.

"Holy Mother of God!"

The bulb hanging from the ceiling was lit, and Jake saw, standing above him, a burly Irishman, his raised eyebrows like woolly caterpillars, his blue eyes bulging.

Jake jumped to his feet. He tried to run but tripped over the long robe and landed with a thud on the carpet. The man stepped on the hem of the robe, pinning him to the floor.

Jake thought fast. Priests have to forgive you if you sin. That's the rule. "Forgive me, Father," he whined.

The big man began to laugh. "You take me for a priest, do you?" He lifted his foot off the bottom of the robe. "Then you don't belong around here, or you'd know I'm just the sexton. But you better get yourself into your own clothes and clear out before the father shows up for early Mass." He prodded Jake with his toe. "I mean it." He looked at the scattered wafers on the floor and the half-empty carafe of wine. "Hurry. Dress yourself. I got me work cut out for me here."

Jake stood up and let the robe drop to the floor. The man ignored his nakedness and concentrated on picking up the mess the boy had made. Giuliano's clothes were still damp, but it couldn't be helped. Jake put them on though they were clammy and just the touch of them pained his back and legs. If the sexton had seen the marks on the boy's body, he didn't mention them, but he did say, "If you need something to eat, boy, go to the back door of the rectory. My wife is the cook here. She'll give you a bite."

Tempted as Jake was by the mention of food, he thought it better not to hang around. No need to press his luck. He mumbled his thanks to the sexton and made his way out into the sanctuary and down the aisle. Just before he got to the huge wooden doors, he remembered the box where people dropped coins for the needy. Well, who was needier than he? The lock was flimsy and easily broken. The box was filled mostly with pennies, but he scooped up all the money and loaded it into his pockets. At least he'd eat for a few days.

Five

Joe Ettor Comes to Town

I T WAS SATURDAY MORNING, but the streets were quiet. By now, Jake was sure, if people were going to work, they would be up and stirring, even though the winter sun had not yet fully risen. He passed a grocer's shop with a dim light glowing. Inside, someone was sweeping the floor. He thought about going in, just to get out of the cold, but he'd been in that shop before and the owner had chased him away for stealing fruit. Even though he now had pennies jangling in his pocket, and he was freezing in his damp clothes, he didn't go in. Better to try someplace where he wasn't known. He headed on down Haverhill Street, past the wide common, where he often slept in summer. It was covered with an inch or so of dirty snow this morning. There should be something open on Jackson Street.

He found a baker and tried the door. It was locked, but there was a clerk inside, arranging loaves on the counter. Jake banged on the door, and the girl looked up, annoyed. "Not open yet!" she called. He reached into his pocket and pulled out three pennies. Nobody in this town was ever closed if there was money to be made. Sure enough, as soon as she saw the money, she came over and unlocked the door.

He pushed past her into the store. It wasn't very warm, but it was dry and out of the wind.

The girl let out some expletive in a foreign language.

"What?" Jake asked roughly.

"You're wet and . . . and . . ."

"Bloody?"

She looked frightened.

"I was in the strike yesterday. I got beat by a cop."

She shook her head sympathetically. "Come in the back where the oven is. It's warm."

She got a bun from under the counter. Jake's stomach rumbled at the sight of it, but he made himself wait. Sometimes, if you were patient . . .

She led him to a room filled with the sweet smell of bread baking and pulled a chair up to a huge brick oven. "Sit down," she said, handing him the bun. "Would you like some coffee, too?"

"I can pay."

"Later," she said.

Polish, he decided. Although he could usually spot an Italian—working, as he did, with so many of them, and the Irish looked like nobody else—he had a hard time telling the rest of these foreigners apart. He stood up to drink his coffee and eat his bun, turning around so his backside could dry as well as his front. He would have been perfectly satisfied, warm room, fresh bread, except he knew how badly stained his borrowed garments still were, despite his attempts in the church. The girl had been kind, and the baker himself only grunted in his direction and kept on with his work. But he couldn't very well ask for soap and water and someplace where he could strip naked and try once more to wash out the rusty stains.

Then he realized that if the police excuse had worked so well on a stranger, it was sure to work on Angelo and his friends, who expected nothing better of cops who would turn fire hoses on strikers in the freezing cold of winter.

Now warm and dry, he thanked the girl for her kindness and left the bakery. He didn't offer to pay for the bun and coffee, but she hadn't asked, had she? No need to waste his little cache of pennies.

The tenement where Angelo lived was just off Union Street. Jake climbed the stairs and knocked on the door. Angelo answered. "Hey, Jake!" he said. "Where you been?" He pulled him into the apartment.

"Hey, Giuliano," he yelled through to the kitchen. "Your clothes are back."

Giuliano circled Jake suspiciously. "What the hell you do to my nice shirt?"

"I—I got beat."

"Those blasted cops! Beating a kid," Angelo said. "Come on, boys, it's late. We gotta go stop them scabs." The men jumped up from the kitchen table. "You stay here, Jake. Wash up. Get some rest."

"And get that blood outa my good shirt!"

When the apartment was empty, Jake found his own clothes, now dry, and exchanged them for Giuliano's stained ones. Like most of the tenement apartments, this one had the bedrooms at the front and back of the house, and the kitchen in the center. The men, having no families to feed, had money for coal, so the kitchen was warm. Jake lay down on the floor, close to the iron stove, and fell asleep. Let the others strike and carry on. He would take care of himself.

He woke with a start. The fire in the stove had long since gone out, and he was stiff from lying on the wooden floor. Why hadn't he gotten into Angelo's bed? He must be crazy, passing up a good chance to lie in a comfortable bed. He examined Giuliano's clothes. He wouldn't get the blood out of the shirt if he scrubbed from now till Christmas. The pants were black, so the stain didn't show, but the white shirt was rusty with the blood he'd tried to wash out. He folded it up so the worst of the stain was underneath and hardly visible. Giuliano would be mad, but how could Jake help it? Maybe the man would blame the police more than he'd blame Jake. If not, so what? Giuliano was rich enough to buy himself another shirt, wasn't he? Still, maybe it would be better not to be here when the men returned. Angelo was good at explanations. Let him do it.

He went down the rickety stairs to the outside door. While he slept, the city had come to life. Union Street seemed to be crawling with people. He'd go north, he decided, away from the mills, away from the river and his father, away from Giuliano's unhappiness. The weather was bitter as he headed up Union Street with no place to go. He had used up all the refuges he knew—the big Catholic church of the Irish, the bakery, Angelo's—better to just keep walking. He turned off into a narrow street lined with mill-owned tenement houses. Women were everywhere, talking excitedly in all their peculiar languages. The words "strike" and "scab" and the name "Ettor" popped out of the foreign words. Angelo had said that he should go hear Ettor speak at the Italian hall tonight, but Giuliano might still be mad. He'd better not go. Still, he was curious. Who was this guy the men all waited for so eagerly?

Actually, he was bored. He had no desire to join the picket lines down by the mills, although he knew that was where the excitement was, if there was any to be had. He was tired of excitement—the kind that meant you got hosed down with freezing water, anyway. He'd steal something, but that seemed stupid when he had pennies rattling in his pocket. So he just walked around the Plains, winding in and out of the narrow alleyways where the garbage was piled. It didn't stink so much in winter. He watched the women. His own mother, long dead . . . would she have been like these foreign women, their heads wrapped in dirty shawls, talking so fast that spit came out of their mouths with the words? No, she was poor, but she was native-born. There was a huge difference, wasn't there? Some of these women carried infants tucked into their shawls and had toddlers clinging to their skirts—dirty kids, all of them, with chilblains and chapped faces. But at least they had mothers, which made him envy them, although he didn't recognize the feeling well enough to name it. He passed the tenement where he'd once spent the night. That funny little shoe girl—what was she doing now that the strike was on?

"Hey, Jake!" He turned abruptly to see who in the Plains might have hailed him. This was foreigners' territory. He dimly recognized the face of the boy who had called out to him. Those few months when he'd been in and out of that awful school learning nothing—yes, it was someone from Newbury Street School. It wasn't one of the boys at work.

"Saw that hose blow you down. Holy Mother, what a sight!"

It was one of the Irish, Jake was sure of that. What was *he* doing in the Plains?

"Don't you remember me? Joe O'Brien—from Newbury School."

"Oh, yeah." Jake wasn't in the mood for schoolboys.

"Are you still on strike?"

"Well, I ain't no scab!"

"Thatta boy."

It made him furious. This shanty Irish schoolboy patting him on the head for striking. What did he know about slaving in the mill? Choking on the dust? Risking your limbs in the machinery and getting paid pennies to do it? He turned away and began to walk fast.

"Hey, I'm talking to you." The boy skipped to catch up. "Where you going to picket today?"

"I gotta go to the hall and get me orders," Jake growled.

"Can I go, too?"

"Strikes ain't child's play." He left Joe standing in the street staring after him with a look that could only mean respect on his wide face.

Jake sniffed. He was somebody. A striker. A real man.

Sunday dawned gray and snowy. The whole household was up and stirring. Rosa rolled over to the middle of the bed. It was still warm in the trough left by Granny J.'s body. She didn't want to get out of bed. The flat would be cold—there was barely enough money to buy coal to cook with and certainly not enough to make the stove warm enough to heat the apartment. She pulled her clothes up from where she kept them at the bottom of the bed and put them on under the covers—all but her worn shoes. She remembered the strange boy in the trash heap and smiled in spite of herself. She had been very brave that night, hadn't she? A little crazy, but really quite brave. And she had done a good deed—not one she could ever brag about, but it *was* a good deed, bringing that poor boy in out of the cold.

She made her morning trip to the toilet down the hall, holding her nose against the stench. The landlord—who was, in fact, Mr. Billy Wood, although, of course, he had an agent to oversee the tenements—was supposed to keep the toilets working well, but none of them did. At least the tap water was still running in the kitchen sink. The pipe hadn't frozen yet.

"Well, good morning, Mees Sleepy One," Mrs. J. said when Rosa appeared at the kitchen door. The women were clustered around the kitchen table, Mrs. J. and Granny had the two chairs, and Mamma the stool. Ricci was clinging to a rung of the stool, as though he didn't trust his thin, little legs. Anna and Marija were leaning against the wall eating their bread and molasses. Rosa couldn't tell if anyone had bothered to go to early Mass. Was this what happened when people went on strike? They forgot everything else, God included?

"Oh, Rosa," Anna said. "You should have been there! Joe Ettor is the handsomest man you've ever seen."

Marija giggled.

"He went to all the halls and talked to everyone about the strike! It was so exciting."

"He talk good Italian," Mamma said. "Better than me." She gave a laugh that ended in a cough.

"No good Liduanian," said Mrs. J. "But no matter—very good look." She winked at Anna, who smiled, and at Marija, who blushed as though someone had mentioned a sweetheart.

"Then how he speak to you?" Mamma asked.

"He speak English, Mr. Aidas do same word in Liduanian. Very good speak. Everyone yell big."

Rosa could tell no one was thinking of going to Mass. "Here, Rosa—" Mamma got up from the stool, Ricci grabbing at her skirt. "Here, Rosa, eat your bread."

"I can't eat yet," Rosa said. "I'm going to Mass, but I guess no one else is."

She hadn't meant for the words to come out quite so prissily. It was almost Miss Finch's voice in her mouth, only Miss Finch, not being Catholic, wouldn't be talking about Mass. She thought that Catholicism was almost as bad as atheism.

"Granny J. went to Mass," Marija said. "The priest

just yelled about strikers, so Ma and I decided not to go."

"We go with you, Rosa," Mamma said. "Father Milanese, he not like Father O'Reilly, he on our side. Come on, Anna, we take Communion with our Rosa." She picked up Ricci, who clutched her around the neck.

"But you've already eaten breakfast—" Rosa was alarmed at Mamma's impiety. "You can't take Communion—"

"I think God don' call bite of stale bread and smear of molasses real food, and what do priest know?"

Why had she brought up the subject of Mass? The mood Mamma was in, she didn't seem to care if she damned her soul to everlasting fire.

Father Milanese didn't condemn the strike. The owners were being unreasonable, he said, speeding up machines to make more profit while cutting wages. Mamma nodded her agreement all through the homily. But then Father Milanese went on to warn them against Joe Ettor, who was an outside agitator, an anarchist, and therefore someone whose motives must be questioned. When he said this, Mamma humphed, got up, and walked out, her shawl, which she'd wrapped around Ricci, trailing in the aisle. Anna ran to join her. There was nothing for Rosa to do but follow. She needn't have worried about Mamma receiving the host in a state of sin.

Outside the church, crowds were gathering, already

planning the next move. Mamma handed Ricci over to Rosa—"Go home, Rosa. Get yourself some bread. Anna and me got work to do."

They came back hours later, exultant. "Some of the men grabbed the hoses and turned them against the watchmen at the mill!" Anna said.

"Now *they* know how it feels to be soaked," Mamma said.

Marija and Mrs. J. came in minutes later even more excited. "You know what your frien' Miz Marino do?" Mrs. J. asked.

"What did that crazy one do?" Mamma was smiling happily.

"She and her friends, dey pull da clothes off a policeman on da bridge and say dey going to trow him in icy river—see how it feels, dey say."

"No!" Mamma said.

"No, some more police come save da poor fool yust in time."

"Mr. Joe Ettor say 'No violence,' last night," Mamma said. "Mrs. Marino better behave, I think."

"It was like a joke, Mamma," Anna said. "You're laughing yourself."

Mamma *was* laughing. It shamed Rosa to see it. Mamma was turning into one of the ignorant immigrants Miss Finch railed against. Her sweet, loving mamma was going to turn into loud, crazy Mrs. Marino, and there was nothing Rosa could do to stop her.

Granny J. didn't leave Rosa enough room to toss and turn in bed, but that night her mind churned. At the strike meeting that evening it was announced that the governor had called up the militia. He'd even given Harvard College boys guns and uniforms. Tomorrow a virtual army would be on the streets of Lawrence, ready to confront any who dared continue the strike. It only made the women more determined than ever. No one was going back to work until the strikers' demands were met, no matter what the governor said or did. *Holy Mother, there was bound to be violence.* How could Rosa save Mamma and Anna from this madness?

That was when Rosa had her great idea. She wouldn't go to school. She'd have her own strike. She'd refuse to go to school as long as Mamma refused to go to work. Then Mamma would see that she *had* to work—that all she and Papa had done to make it possible for at least Rosa to get an education would be wasted. Mamma couldn't stand waste, so she'd realize that she had to go back to work for Papa's sake, if not Rosa's.

Six

Songs of Defiance

MAMMA WAS PINCHING Rosa's toes. "Wake, up, *dormigliona*. Time for school."

"I'm not going to school," Rosa said, burrowing under the quilt. The bed felt luxurious when Granny J. wasn't in it with her. "I made up my mind, Mamma. If you and Anna go on strike, I go on strike."

Mamma threw back her head and laughed. It struck Rosa that she had heard Mamma's laugh more in the last couple of days than she had since before Papa died. "Okay, *Signorina Asino*. You win. No school today." She patted Rosa's toes. "See you later on. Me and Anna got to go now to join the march."

Rosa could have screamed. She was not a donkey. What was the matter with Mamma? *She* was the stubborn one. She was supposed to give in, go to work, do anything to keep her child in school. Rosa sat up and threw off the quilt, but before she could open her mouth to argue further, Mamma, Anna, Mrs. J., and Marija had walked through her room and out the front door. She could hear them laughing as they clattered down the stairs. They were probably laughing at her. Miss Donkey, indeed! She musn't be late. She jumped up and put on her clothes, grabbed a bit of bread off the kitchen table, and left the flat.

The street was full of women and girls, all heading toward Jackson Street. She slipped in and out among them until she got to Jackson Street herself. It was there she finally saw Mamma and Anna . . . and yet, it was not Mamma she saw. The woman she saw was drawn up to a height much taller than her squat little mamma. Her face was red with cold and rage, and then she began to laugh—*laugh*—right in the face of one of the Harvard boys the governor had called into service. Even in his new wool militia uniform and with his shiny rifle he looked as frightened as a three-year-old caught in some mischief.

Finally, he brought down his rifle so the tip of the barrel poked Mamma's shawl. Rosa's hand flew to her mouth. He wouldn't kill her! How could some silly college boy kill her mamma? Still, he was so scared, who could tell what he might do? And then Mamma did a strange thing. She began to sing.

The boy, his face full of confusion, backed up and let her pass, let all the women pass, so that they began to march like a ragged army down Jackson Street. They

gathered in strength as they went, for women were pouring out of every doorway to join them. They took up
Mamma's song. Where had the song come from? Where
had Mamma learned to sing about workers uniting? The
only songs Rosa had ever heard her sing were Italian lull-
abies and arias from Verdi and Puccini. Those songs had
died with Papa. But every woman on the street seemed to
know this song. It was not just the Italian women but the
Lithuanians and Poles and Syrians and Turks and Jews—
all the polyglot female residents of the Plains, singing in
many languages but together in one thunderous voice.

It was not only Mamma's college boy who was
scared. The newly arrived militia and weary local police
stationed along the route fell back as the crowd of
women swelled. There were girl workers like Anna, too,
of course, but there were also children smaller than Rosa
and babies in their mothers' arms. One of the babies,
looking back over its mother's shoulder, stared at Rosa
with big brown eyes, as if to say: "Why has my mamma
gone mad? Where is she taking me?"

They were heading toward the common. Rosa, careful not to make herself part of the actual parade, clung to
the buildings, somehow compelled to shadow the line of
marchers until they reached the common, where they
merged with hundreds of people already milling about
on the snowy ground.

Rosa had just found a spot on the edge of the crowd

when a band struck up and the mass of people began to sing—not Mamma's song but a different one, this one in English. A thrill went through Rosa's body. How did everyone know the words? How did they know the English? The tune was easy. It was one they sang at school, to Mrs. Julia Ward Howe's "Battle Hymn of the Republic," but these words were not "Glory! Glory! Hallelujah" but something about solidarity and the union.

There was an improvised platform at the end of the common closest to Jackson Street. There in the center of a group of men, whom she knew by their worn clothes to be workers, was a stranger with a bright red bow tie sticking out of his overcoat. The crowd roared at the sight of him. "Ettor! Ettor!" they cried. So this was the dangerous Joe Ettor. He seemed hardly threatening to Rosa. He was not so tall as Papa had been, but he did have the same mass of curly dark hair, and he smiled at the marchers as he raised his hands for silence. Immediately, the crowd was still, and Rosa could hear his voice ringing in the cold air.

"We will march down to the mills," he said. "And they will meet us in force. The governor is so afraid of us that he has called out the militia, including these beardless Harvard boys. But they cannot weave cloth with bayonets!" The crowd roared its approval. He held up his hands again for silence. "My fellow workers, by all means make this strike as peaceful as possible. In the last analysis, all the blood spilled will be your blood. And above all, remember they can defeat us only if they can separate us into nationalities or skills. If we hold together no matter what they do or threaten to do, no one can defeat us. Not even the governor of Massachusetts and his thousands of militia men and Harvard boys."

He spoke more, in languages Rosa could not understand, but others could, for there were more roars of approval. "Division is the surest means to lose this strike. Never forget! Among workers there is only one nationality, one race, one creed. Remember always that you are workers with interests against those of the mill owners. There are but two races: the race of useful members of society and the race of useless ones. Never forget that in our cause solidarity is necessary."

"Solidarity!" a voice cried out, and the word ricocheted about the great common. "Solidarity forever!" Another word besides "Short pay! All out!" and the words to the songs that everyone in the crowd knew either in English or in their native tongues.

"Now let's join our brothers and sisters already at the picket lines!" Joe Ettor cried, and the crowd, roaring and singing another new song, began to move out from the common, heading down Jackson toward Canal Street.

> *"We shall not be, we shall not be moved.*
> *We shall not be, we shall not be moved."*

Mamma and Anna were in the first line of marchers, but they didn't notice Rosa standing at the edge of the common. Someone had given Anna a huge American flag, which she was holding high above her head. Rosa found herself melting into the crowd. There was something burning inside her that wanted to march, that wanted to sing. She wished she had a flag like Anna's to wave high above her head as she walked.

What would Miss Finch think of her now? Her star pupil caught up in the excitement of the mob, seduced by the outside agitator, the anarchist Ettor? She would be alarmed and deeply disappointed, Rosa knew. But at that moment, the snow falling heavily and covering her hair—she'd forgotten her thin worsted cap—she felt no longer alone but a part of something huge and powerful and right. Yes, at that moment, no one could have persuaded her that what she and the thousands about her were doing was wicked. No. Like Mamma said, it was better to fight and starve than to work and starve.

And then she saw them at the bottom of the hill: not a single frightened Harvard boy or even the familiar Lawrence policemen but a veritable army of militia, dressed in their heavy blue woolen uniforms and leather boots. No danger that *they* would feel the snow and the cold. Their guns, with the swordlike bayonets attached, were pointed directly at the line of marchers.

There was a jostling in the crowd, and the singing

trailed off, as if the cold steel of the bayonets pointed at their bodies had brought them back from the joy of the parade to the deadly seriousness of the threat they were facing.

Cries and jeers rose up behind Rosa, and she saw that members of the crowd were breaking away, some heading east toward the Prospect and Everett mills and others west toward the Atlantic and Pacific mills. She could feel the stir about her, rather like the classroom when Miss Finch left the room, and it frightened her. She wanted to get out of the middle of these thousands of restless bodies and go home, but she couldn't move; she was trapped by marchers pressing this way and that about her. She couldn't see over the heads of the people around her, though she could see the top of the flag and knew it meant that Mamma and Anna must be standing right in front of the armed militia. If the crowd pushed too hard . . . ? She wanted to cry out a warning to Mamma, to Anna, to everyone. *What are you doing here? They will kill you. You're nothing to them! Nothing!* But the screams were strangled in her tight throat.

The singing had stopped entirely. The marchers in front of the Washington Mill were so quiet that Rosa could hear the shouts and screams from far down Canal Street. What was happening there? Then a whisper swept through the crowd. *They've stabbed a boy! They've stabbed a boy!* She thought for a moment that she might faint and realized, if she were to, she'd never fall to the street. There was no room. She was suffocating. She had to get out of this trap of bodies. She had to go home.

Then someone began to sing:

> "*Like a tree planted by the water,*
> *We shall not be moved.*"

Another voice shouted, rather than sang, "Let him call out his militia!"

"*We shall not be moved,*" the marchers responded.

"Let them shoot and stab us," another voice said.

"*We shall not be moved.*"

And everyone around her was singing now:

> "*We shall not be, we shall not be moved.*
> *We shall not be, we shall not be moved.*
> *Like a tree planted by the water,*
> *We shall not be moved.*"

The singing went on and on. Above it, she could hear the bull horn–amplified demands that the crowd disperse. There were occasional scuffles when someone tried to work his or her way through the marchers toward the mills. "Scab! Scab! Go home!"

Eventually, Rosa could feel that the crowd had loosened its grip on her. She began to ease her way sideways until she was able to slip out of the crowd and into a side street, where she found herself suddenly looking up at the dark brick exterior of Newbury Street School.

She was panting, not from running—she hadn't run at all—but from the exertion of working her way through the mob. Her heart was pounding, and despite the snow, which swirled about her and almost obscured the school building, she was sweating as though it were summer.

Later, she wondered why she had done it, but at the moment the school represented safety, and unlike the marchers whose courage had nearly suffocated her, she wanted to be safe from those soldiers with their fixed bayonets that stabbed and, who knew? might shoot children.

"You're tardy, Rosa," Miss Finch said as Rosa crept into the classroom.

Rosa ducked her head in apology and slid into her seat. There were only a handful of students present. The native-born and the Irish were there, except for Joe O'Brien, but not many of the children of the unskilled workers, the ones who would be on strike. The class was in the middle of their arithmetic lesson. Fortunately, arithmetic came easily to Rosa, and although she had no textbook, she had been able to keep up by listening carefully to Miss Finch's explanations.

When it was nearly time for the dinner bell, Miss

Finch said, "There is, as you no doubt know, a large, unruly mob on Canal Street. I suggest that when you go home for dinner you avoid going in that direction no matter how curious you might feel about the activities taking place today. The crowd is dangerous. Some are undoubtedly armed. If you are wise, you'll remain in the safety of the school building this dinner hour, as I will myself. But since some of your parents may be expecting you home, I won't prevent your going. Just stay away from the mill area and try to stay out of trouble."

Rosa hadn't thought about what she should do at dinnertime. Would anyone be expecting her home? Granny J. was probably there with baby Ricci and Mrs. J.'s little boys. But she'd have to go back on the street to get home. She got up and started for the door only to be stopped by the teacher's voice calling her name.

"Rosa."

"Yes, Miss Finch."

"You were absent Friday afternoon. Do you have an excuse for that?"

"No, ma'am."

The teacher stood up and came to where Rosa waited. "You must not let your parents—your mother, rather—keep you from school. You understand that, don't you?" she said softly.

"Yes, ma'am."

"I hope you were able to persuade her not to strike."

Rosa just hung her head. Miss Finch's shoes were almost new—leather boots laced tight. Her feet would never feel the snow leaking through the soles.

"Rosa, I'm speaking to you, dear. Look at me, please."

She raised her eyes to look at the teacher's pale face pinched in disapproval. It was thin, but had Miss Finch ever known real hunger?

"Are the people in your family a part of this terrible strike?"

"They're hungry, Miss Finch." Rosa nearly whispered the words, but the teacher had heard her. She could see Miss Finch's eyes blink, and she began to fiddle with a pencil she held.

"You know what Mr. Wood said. The mills can't afford to pay wages for fifty-six hours' work when they're only getting fifty-four."

Something stiffened inside of Rosa. "But he got five houses."

"He *has* five houses."

"Yes, ma'am. And so many automobiles he can't count them."

Miss Finch jerked her head. Her cheeks reddened. "I think that was meant as a jest. Nonetheless. Your parents are breaking the law."

"My papa is dead."

"Yes, you said. I'm sorry. Truly. But whoever in your household is taking part in this wretched business needs to be warned off. Do they realize that Joseph Ettor is an anarchist? That means, Rosa, that he doesn't believe either in God or the law. He's"—she lowered her voice and her head and said, almost in a whisper—"he's a *Marxist*."

"Father Milanese says we have the right to ask for a living wage."

Miss Finch sniffed. "Father Milanese is not in line with the rest of the religious leaders of this city, all of whom have denounced the strike as godless and lawless. Isn't he Italian?"

"Yes, ma'am."

"There, you see. I'm sure your bishop will soon set him straight."

There was no need to remind Miss Finch that she, Rosa, was also Italian, as was her entire family. Despite the two strikes against her—that she was both Catholic and Italian—Miss Finch had always encouraged her.

"Well, I had hopes for you, Rosa." She walked away and put the pencil down on the desk, expecting, perhaps, that Rosa would disappear.

"Please, ma'am. I want to learn. You said I should make something of myself."

The teacher came back and put her hand gently on Rosa's shoulder. "Yes, I did. I'm just—I'm just afraid for you, Rosa, dear. There are so many obstacles. . . ."

"Yes, ma'am."

"Try to persuade your mother not to strike, won't

you? It's a terrible mistake. Those outside agitators . . .
They can't be trusted."

"He said no violence. That's what he told everybody."

"Who said that?"

"Mr. Ettor."

Miss Finch's hand went from Rosa's shoulder to her
own throat. "He's the worst. Rosa, you mustn't believe
anything he says. He doesn't care for the mills or the
workers here in Lawrence. He is only after power for himself. There'll be terrible violence. He'll do awful things
and try to blame others. People will get killed. You'll see."

Rosa left the school. She should have run, there was so
little time before the afternoon session, but the streets were
too crowded for her to run properly, and, besides, she
needed to think. Could Miss Finch be right? Could the
man Mamma and Anna and all the workers were following
be only after power for himself? A boy had been stabbed
this morning. But it was the militia who had done it, not
the workers. Unless . . . unless Miss Finch was right. Unless
Joe Ettor would try to blame the police and the militia for
things his own followers had done. Rosa shook her head to
try to clear it. Everything was too confusing. Whom could
she believe? It was a messy, terrible business. She wanted
her mother and sister out of it no matter who was right and
who was wrong. It was just too dangerous. Suppose they
got killed and she was left alone with only little Ricci?
They'd starve for sure—if they didn't freeze first.

Seven

The Return of Rosa's Rat

R OSA WENT BACK to school on Tuesday. What else was she to do? Mamma and Anna and the Jarusalises were so involved in the strike that they were always out, meeting, picketing, or marching. She'd tried to convince them how dangerous it was until she was hoarse, but Mamma just patted her on the head and went out the door. Granny J. was busy with her grandsons, Jonas and Kestutis, and little Ricci, and Rosa couldn't talk to her anyway.

The big news at school was that Joe O'Brien had been arrested. "Arrested?" Rosa said. "Why?"

"Oh, he wanted to be a big shot. He went down to the picket line, where a bunch of strikers were throwing snowballs at the police. They took 'em all to jail." Luigi was grinning. "But Joe's got him a Irish daddy. He hauled Joe home and said he couldn't leave the house till the strike was over. He was lucky. The judge give the men a year."

"For throwing snowballs?"

Luigi nodded solemnly. "For throwing snowballs."

When Miss Finch walked into the classroom, the straggly remnant of what had once been the class stood up. They weren't always so polite, but the strike had infused a bit of pride into the children of the strikers.

Miss Finch smiled faintly at the gesture. "You may be seated, class," she said.

"You hear about Joe, miss?" Luigi asked.

"Yes," she said and hesitated, as though undecided as to how to proceed.

"He almost went to jail!" Celina said.

"Joseph was very foolish," Miss Finch said. "And, although it is a shame that he will be missing so much school, I think his father is wise to keep him off the streets. I trust this will be a lesson to you all—if you had any thought of becoming involved in this ugly business."

Rosa winced.

"I'm sure some of you think a year in jail is an unreasonable sentence for throwing snowballs. But as the judge said, 'The only way we can teach them is to deal out the severest sentences.' It should certainly make other Italian strikers think twice before they show such disrespect to authority."

"Joe ain't Italian," Luigi said.

"And he should have known better. Now, those of you who have arithmetic books . . ."

But Rosa couldn't put her mind on sums. What if Anna were arrested? After all, she had been right up front in the parade with her big American flag. The police were sure to notice her, and Anna wouldn't be able to stand being in jail for a day, much less a year. Or Mamma, who had been singing louder than anybody? Her heart skipped a beat. If Mamma were arrested, none of them could survive. She had to persuade Mamma to go back to work. Or at the very least to stop marching and picketing.

That evening she tried again. "Mamma, they put some men in jail—for a whole year. Just for throwing snowballs."

Mamma sighed. "They tell us law show no favorite, but how can you say that? Put a man in jail for throwing snowball."

"What if they put you in jail?"

"Who, me?" Mamma laughed. "Me? I just stupid Italian woman. What do they care about me?"

"*Mamma!* They'll put anyone in jail for the least little thing."

"Can they put ten, twenty thousand peoples in jail? Only jail big enough is the mills, and we already been in those."

Mrs. J., Anna, and Marija laughed at that. Anna laughed so hard, she began to cough. Mamma got her a cup of water and put her arm around her. She murmured to Anna while the girl sipped the water. Rosa watched in horror. Was it just the winter weather or was Anna getting sick in the lungs the way so many of the girls did?

She was startled by Mrs. J.'s jovial "And we ain't goin' back till dey do what we say, hey, Alba?" Mrs. J. had taken to calling Mamma by her first name. Mamma looked up, her worried look gone. It wasn't right. The Jarusalises were boarders whose no-good papa had run off. Now all of a sudden, Mrs. J. was acting cozy as a sister to Mamma, and Mamma didn't even seem to mind. She was smiling.

"Oof," she said, dropping into a chair. "My feet tired, just like I work all day. Go down street, Marija. Find out where we meet tomorrow." Anna started for the door. "No, not you, *bambina*. You rest a bit here with Mamma. We got to be strong for tomorrow."

"Mamma!" Rosa couldn't believe her ears. "You're not going to parade again *tomorrow*?"

"I do if Joe Ettor say so."

"Mamma, you're just letting those godless anarchists push you around!"

Mamma snapped around to look at her. "What do you know, Rosa? You see inside Mr. Joe Ettor's heart?"

"Miss Finch—"

"Don' 'Miss Finch' me, okay? She know school, she don' know nothing 'bout mill work or Mr. Joe Ettor, neither. Now go on, Marija. Run ask Mrs. Marino where we meeting tomorrow morning. And you, Anna, go lie down on the bed a minute." Anna hesitated. "Go on, obey your mamma." Anna went into the back room, but she left the door open, as though afraid she might miss something.

Mamma settled down in her chair, and then to Rosa's horror she leaned forward, took off her worn shoes, and began to rub her feet—right there in front of Mrs. Jarusalis. She breathed out a huge sigh, making Mrs. J. laugh again.

"Goot idea, Alba," she said, taking off her own shoes and raising a big, dirty foot across her knee to rub it, her skirt hiked up almost to her waist.

Was the strike going to turn them all into savages?

"Oooh, could I use a cuppa coffee now," Mamma said.

"Can you still remember da taste?" Mrs. J. asked.

"Never forget coffee. Like you don' forget your first kiss." Mamma's eyes were closed, and she licked her lips, as though tasting either the coffee or the kiss, making Rosa cringe with embarrassment.

"I have to do my homework now."

"Good," said Mamma without opening her eyes. "Good girl."

After she had finished her homework—what she could do of it without an arithmetic or grammar textbook— Rosa stayed in the front room with the door closed. She could hear the women talking and laughing; even Granny and the little Jarusalis boys were joining in the good humor of the evening. Mamma and Mrs. J. were the happiest they'd been since they'd lived together. It made Rosa angry. Mamma was ruining her life—all their lives—with this crazy strike. Anna would get sick, and they'd starve—which reminded her that no one had even mentioned supper.

Just then the door to the hall flew open, and Marija burst through it and headed for the kitchen. "Close the door!" Rosa cried, but Marija didn't hear her. She was rushing in with news. When Rosa got off the bed to close the door herself, she heard them all talking at the same time, their words tripping over each other. Rosa heard the word "food" and, in spite of herself, went to the kitchen to find out what the excitement was about.

Anna was already up from her rest. She turned when she saw Rosa standing there. "They've set up a soup kitchen!" she said, her eyes dancing. "Union workers from Boston and Lowell brought it. And they say people are going to send money from all over the country! Workers everywhere want to support us in the strike!"

Mamma was on her feet. While the girls gathered bowls and spoons for all of them, Mamma went into the back room and took the still sleeping little Ricci out of bed and wrapped him in her shawl. "Come," she ordered. "Everybody to the Italian hall."

Rosa stood aside and let them all pass her. She hung back. At the front door, Mamma turned. "Come, Rosa. You, too."

Rosa hesitated. "It's like begging when you can't pay," she muttered.

"It's like feasting," Mamma said. "Come on, don' be a fool. You need to eat." She reached out her free hand and said gently, "Come on, my Rosina. Don' be sour face."

Rosa didn't take Mamma's hand, but she followed her down the stairs and out into the street. Everyone was in a carnival mood, heading for the various ethnic halls where there was food to be had. "Come on, Marta," Mamma said to Mrs. J. "You come to Chabis Hall. Be Italian just for one night. Too far to walk to Sons of Lithuania, okay?" Mrs. J. laughed and all the J.'s went with them to Chabis Hall, where tables and chairs were set up. They were among the first, and Mamma sent Granny and Rosa and little Ricci and the boys to save seats while the women and older girls stood in line.

The soup was thick with vegetables and bits of meat, the aroma alone almost enough to fill an empty stomach. There was fresh crusty bread, too, more for each person than any of them had had for months. "See, Rosa," Mamma said. "We don' starve if we strike. Our union friends help us."

Rosa didn't answer. Her mouth was full, but she couldn't help wondering what happened when you ate the food of atheists and anarchists. Was it like taking the host when you were in a state of sin? Did you go to hell?

Rosa lay in bed, unable to sleep, the taste of the thick soup still in her mouth. She should never have gone to the hall. When you're hungry, you can so easily be led astray, and they had been led astray. Even the people who had no desire to strike, who only stayed out of work because their fear of the neighbors was greater than their fear of the mill owners—they had gone to the halls and eaten the food sent from the union members in Boston and Lowell, and they had been warmed and filled and they had forgotten to be wary. She flung herself over in bed. Granny J. grunted. She mustn't wake the old woman up. Mamma would be furious with her. If Granny complained, then Mamma and Anna and Ricci would have to give their bed in the back room to the old lady, and the three of them come and share Rosa's already too small bed. But at least they wouldn't snore, not the way Granny did. Jonas and Kestutis, who shared the narrow cot next to the opposite wall, were sleeping peacefully. It hadn't worried them to eat the food of atheists. Only Rosa. Everyone else had just laughed at her fears.

Granny J. turned over, snatching most of the quilt as she did so. Rosa wanted to pull it back, but she knew she mustn't. What would happen when the J.'s stopped paying rent? They would, of course, when they had no earnings. If Mamma stopped paying the rent, would Mr. Wood throw them out into the snow? No. Mr. Wood had once been a mill worker. He knew how it was. He wouldn't be so cruel. . . . Or would he?

The questions inside her head were so noisy that she almost didn't hear the sound. Then she did. It was the sound of someone knocking ever so gently on the door. She climbed out of bed and tiptoed to the door and put her ear on the keyhole.

"Hey, shoe girl," a voice whispered. "You awake?"

Rosa nodded.

"I say, girl, you there?"

"Oh. Yes. Is it you?"

"Yeah. Can I come in?"

She turned the key and opened the door a crack. "What are you doing here?"

"Ah, come on," he said. "It's freezing out there. I'll sleep in the kitchen, like before, all right?"

"No, it's not all right," Rosa whispered, looking nervously toward the lump in the bed that was Granny J. "Go home and sleep. I bet your parents don't even know where you are."

"Who you think I'm running from?"

She hadn't thought of that—someone who had to run *away* from home and not toward it.

He was already pushing past her into the room. "I'll be gone before they're awake," he said as he went through

70

to the kitchen. She closed and locked the front door, not knowing what else to do or how to get rid of him.

She wanted to tell him not to take any bread this time, but how could she? She'd had a big bowl of soup and a huge slice of bread all to herself just a few hours before, and besides, the bread left in the kitchen was hard and moldy. Rosa watched him lie down, curling close to the cold stove, with his back to her. She could hear Anna's coughing from the other room. It sent knives through her own chest. She waited a minute before leaving the kitchen. She quietly shut the kitchen door, and then she leaned against it, her heart beating too fast. Why had she let the boy in? She didn't even know his name— all she knew was that he was a thief who had stolen bread from them the last time she'd felt sorry for him and let him sleep in the kitchen. And he'd do it again. She was sure of that. Well, it was too late now. She crept back to bed.

Granny was sprawled all over the bed, so Rosa lay stiffly in the narrow space left to her and recited multiplication tables in her head to keep from thinking about all the things that were bombarding her mind.

Why was Mamma shaking her shoulder? It couldn't be morning yet.

"What is it, Mamma?" She spoke without opening her eyes.

"Shh. Hush. It's Anna, and I don't want to wake anyone up." Anna leaned over and whispered in her ear.
"Who is that guy in the kitchen?"

Rosa was wide awake now. "What guy?"

"What do you mean, 'What guy?' I got up to get a
drink of water and nearly tripped over him. Scared the
life out of me. Come on, Rosa. You know who I mean—
the boy that smells like a canal, who's lying right now on
our kitchen floor."

"Oh, him."

"Yes, *him*. You let him in?"

She nodded, not daring to look Anna in the face,
even in the dark.

"Did you? Then you must know who he is."

"He's—" Oh, dear, she still didn't know his name. "It's
uh . . . Fred—from school."

"Well get Fred or whatever his name is out of here
fast."

"I can't. He's got no place to go. He'd freeze to death
outside."

"Heaven help us, you're right. Well, get him out of
here before Mamma wakes up and catches him, understand?" She sighed. "Now go back to sleep, but make
sure—"

"I will. You, too."

"How can I go back to sleep? My heart is pounding
like a beater on a loom. Such a fright!"

"I'm sorry, okay? I'll get him out early."

"Be sure you do."

But she slept so late, Mamma was pinching her toes and telling her she'd be tardy for school. She sat up quickly. Granny and the little boys were already up and out of the room. She must have slept terribly late. Oh, dear—the boy. She'd promised Anna she'd get him out before Mamma got up.

"Your little rat come again last night," Mamma said as if reading her mind.

"My—what?" Had Mamma seen him, then?

"In and out in the dead of night, taking the last of the bread along."

She couldn't speak. Why was Mamma calling him *her* rat?

"Only this time," Mamma smiled broadly, "he leave a penny behind. Some rat, huh?"

Rosa just lay there blinking in the still-dark room.

"Up, up, Rosina, get yourself up now and run down to the baker and get us some new bread before you go off to school, okay?"

Rosa dressed quickly. Mamma pressed three pennies into her hand. "Tell Mr. Cavacco we good for the rest soon as we win this strike, okay?"

Rosa did as she was told, even though her face felt flushed and she couldn't look directly at Mr. Cavacco when she gave him the three pennies and asked for the other two cents to be put on account. She knew Mamma was trying to stretch out her last pay envelope as long as possible. Mr. Cavacco didn't argue. He took a little notebook from his drawer, pushed his glasses up on his forehead, licked his tiny stub of a pencil, and wrote down carefully on the page headed MRS. SERUTTI: "January 17, 2 cents due."

When she brought the new loaf home, it was greeted with squeals of delight. Mamma got the big knife and cut nine thin, perfectly straight slices, coated each one with a smear of molasses, and passed seven of them to the waiting household. She took the two soft slices from the middle of the loaf and cut one of them up into tiny squares for Ricci. He stuffed a handful into his mouth and chewed the bread with a look of serious determination. Mamma smiled at him, leaving her own slice untouched in case the baby needed it as well. *He needs milk.* Rosa's heart hurt for her brother. When she was small, she'd had milk almost every day. Back when Papa was alive.

There was another parade that day, and there was, as Miss Finch had predicted, some violence. The strikers threw ice at the militia, and the militia retaliated by beating the strikers with the backs of their swords. "Nobody was hurt, little Rosa," Mamma said. "Stop your worry.

Your mamma and Anna are fine. You should see that girl. When anybody raise their gun, she wrap that big flag all around her. They don' dare shoot the flag, those Harvard boys!" Mamma laughed.

There was an even better parade on Thursday. Mr. Marad, who had a dye shop on Oak Street, led it with his big Syrian band. "Oh, it was very grand," Mamma said. "Best band yet."

Then the very next day, the police got a tip. There was dynamite stored in Mr. Marad's shop. They raided it and, sure enough, found the dynamite. Mr. Marad protested that he had no idea how it got there. Joe Ettor swore that the mill owners had paid someone to plant it and then blame it on the strikers. The city was in an uproar, with each side blaming the other. More dynamite was found, some in the cemetery and some in a shoe shop right next door to the radical printing shop where Joe Ettor went every day to collect his mail. The authorities were both outraged and triumphant. Didn't the dynamite prove what they had contended from the beginning—that nothing but violence and disorder would result from this illegal strike?

Rosa was desperate. "Mamma, please. If they are storing dynamite . . ."

"Who is storing dynamite! Nobody, I say. It'sa Mr. Billy Wood'sa monkey tricks!" The madder Mamma got, the less American she sounded.

"You don't know that, Mamma, not for sure."

Mamma looked at Rosa, her nostrils flaring. "Don' believe everything that teacher say, Rosa. She don' know the heart of Mr. Billy Wood like I do."

"She *does* know Mr. Wood. She said so. He used to be a worker himself. He really cares about workers."

"Rosa! Look at this apartment! He give us this—we only pay little rent, yes? He so kind heart to us he give me six dollar twenty-five cent a week for work and take back six dollar for rent. Oh, yes, he got big heart for me. Him with his six house and so many cars he don' count how many. Oh, yes, sir, he care so much about his people in the mills." She stopped only long enough to catch her breath. "You know why dynamite found in Mr. Marad's shop—huh, you know?" She didn't wait for an answer. "Because Mr. Marad lead best parade yet with his big Syrian band is why. Now he in jail. No more good band for parade. That's all Mr. Billy Wood think. He don' care innocent man in jail."

Rosa shrank back. Sometimes she was as frightened by Mamma's rage as she was by the events happening in the streets.

School became a kind of refuge. Even though Miss Finch never failed to condemn the strike, Rosa could almost close her ears to that and focus her anxieties on performing well in arithmetic and history and, above all, in

English. She *would* be an American, an educated, civilized, respected American, not a despised child of an immigrant race. When she grew up, she'd change her name and marry a real American and have real American children. She wouldn't go out to work in a mill and leave them in the care of someone's old granny who couldn't even speak English. She'd stay home herself and cook American food and read them American books and . . . But even as she thought these determined thoughts, somewhere in the back of her mind she could smell rigatoni smothered in tomato sauce with bits of sausage in it and could hear her mamma's beautiful voice singing *Un Bel Di*.

Eight

Bread and Rosa

To Rosa's relief, the boy didn't come knocking again. When Mamma asked about him, Rosa said something vague—"He wasn't in school today"—something even Father Milanese couldn't classify as a lie. She didn't want to lay one more sin upon her soul on his account. She went to confession on Saturday and got the first lie off her conscience, the one about knowing him from school, so that she could take Communion. She went to Mass alone. Mamma and Anna were too busy meeting and parading. She came home feeling as though an icicle had pierced straight through to her belly. She was cold and hungry, but it wasn't just that. She was angry. Why should she have to carry the burden of piety for the whole household? It was as though the strike had become their religion, with Joe Ettor their priest.

As soon as she stepped into the apartment, Rosa could hear the excited babble of women's voices coming from the kitchen. Even when there was momentary quiet for one voice to speak, the words were immediately interpreted in a noisy tangle of languages, louder than the roar of water over the river dam. The door between the front room and the kitchen was open, and over the racket she could hear Mrs. Marino's shrill voice speaking in such rapid Italian that she had to strain to understand. She assumed at first that Mrs. Marino's excitement was over Arturo Giovannitti, who had arrived to help Joe Ettor. Mr. Giovannitti was Mrs. Marino's new enthusiasm. She liked him even better than everyone else's hero, Mr. Ettor, because Mr. Giovannitti was a poet, and unlike the American-born Mr. Ettor, he had come straight from the old country, where, Mrs. Marino knew for a fact, he'd been one step ahead of the police, who were going to jail him for being an anarchist. *Come è romantico!* she had exclaimed, pressing her hands to her large bosom.

But it wasn't Mr. Giovannitti she was enthusing about now. Someone new was coming that night on the train. Someone more important than either Ettor or Giovannitti. Someone, it seemed, more important than the Holy Father, the pope. From the sound of it, more important that our Lord himself.

Rosa plunked down on the edge of her bed and took off her sodden shoes. Her feet were freezing. She rubbed her toes to try to get the circulation going. What she wouldn't give for a new pair of shoes! *I'd sell my soul,* she thought and was immediately seized with panic. No, no, she hadn't meant that!

"Rosa? Is that you?" At least Mamma noticed she was home. Sometimes during the past week, Rosa had wondered if Mamma even knew she was alive—or cared. "Rosa, come here. We need some good schoolgirl English." Reluctantly, Rosa stood up. The floor was cold under her bare, aching feet. "Come on, quick. We need you." Then to the others, "Rosa write good as⸴ schoolteacher, eh, Rosa?" Rosa blushed to hear Mamma bragging.

"Rosina, *bambina!* Coma here!" Mrs. Marino grabbed Rosa to her bosom and kissed her on both cheeks. "Growing up, you are. What grade you go to now?"

"Sixth," Rosa mumbled, embarrassed by the display.

"What she say?" Mrs. Marino asked. "I don'ta hear so good. Too much banging in the mill."

"Six," said Mamma loudly. "First in her class, too."

"That'sa fine girl," Mrs. Marino said, beaming at Rosa and kissing her again soundly. "Now, now, come, come, you sit." She turned to the women occupying the two chairs. "Up, up. Give our schoolgirl a chair." Both women stood. "No, no, not you, Mrs. Petrovsky. You got the bad legs." Mrs. Petrovsky sat down again. "Here, Rosa, right here." She put her hands on Rosa's shoulders and pushed her down on the chair nearer the table.

In front of where Rosa sat was a large white rectangle of pasteboard. Beside the pasteboard was a bottle of ink—her ink, Rosa noted, feeling a twinge of resentment that someone had dared raid her precious school supplies— and a brush about an inch wide.

"Okay," said Mrs. Marino. "You see, we got to make a *beeeeeg* sign for tonight to take to da train station. It got to be good message in vera nice writing. We need you, smart girl, to do it for us, okay?"

Should she tell Mrs. Marino and the others that she hated the strike? That she wanted no part of making a *beeeeeg* sign for it? She should, but she knew she wouldn't. She was such a coward, and Mamma had bragged, so all she said was, "What do you want the sign to say?"

"We thinking. We thinking. Something vera good." All eyes were on Mrs. Marino. Everyone else was quiet. It was a solemn moment. "Okay. Now, you see they give one piece only. So only one sign. So gotta be really, really good. The best sign in parade, eh?"

All the women murmured agreement. *Yes, yes, the best sign.*

Mrs. Marino continued. "We want Mr. Big Bill Haywood see our sign soon he step off the train. We want alla newspaperman from big city New York, from Boston, see our sign." She leaned so close to Rosa that Rosa could smell the old sweat clinging to her dress. "Now, Rosa, you got to write vera big, vera nice letters, so Mr. Big Bill Haywood read them even from train window, right? So he know we is somebody even before he get off the train, okay?"

Rosa nodded. What else was she to do?

"Now, ladies, what we say on our sign?"

For a moment, they were startled. Wasn't it Mrs. Marino's job to come up with all the big ideas? "We say," said Mrs. Jarusalis, hesitantly, one eye on Mrs. Marino, "we say, 'We want bread.' Dat's number one, okay? We gotta have bread."

"*Si, si,*" said Mrs. Marino, plainly disappointed. "But is not good enough. Everyone write that. Is nobody don'ta want bread."

"'We want bread' is goot sign, is true sign," Mrs. Petrovsky protested shyly. The others murmured in agreement, but Mrs. Marino pinned Rosa's right wrist to the table, lest she think the matter was settled and begin to write too soon.

Then Rosa felt a familiar hand rest lightly on her hair and begin to stroke it. She looked up into Mamma's face. The room was silent, watching. Mamma played with a curl on Rosa's shoulder.

"I think," she began quietly, "I think we want . . . not just bread for our bellies. We want more than only bread. We want food for our hearts, our souls. We want—how to say it? We want, you know—Puccini music. . . . We want for our beautiful children some beauty." She leaned over and kissed the curl on her finger. "We want roses. . . ."

There was a murmur while Mamma's words were interpreted for the non-English speakers. Then a ripple of sighs as each understood. Now all the women, even Mrs. Marino, were looking at Mamma with something like awe in their eyes.

Then Anna said, "That's beautiful, Mamma, but it's much too long for our little sign."

Mamma shook her head, as though her mind was coming back from a countryside beyond Naples, where she remembered beauty. "*Si, si,* too long, but Rosa fix it, eh, Rosa?"

Mrs. Marino loosened her grip on Rosa's wrist, and Rosa picked up the brush and reached toward the ink pot. All the women leaned toward the table. She could hear their noisy breathing and smell their fetid clothing.

"No, no," Mrs. Marino shouted, spreading her arms wide. "Back, back! Give her room. Don'ta touch the table! No one!" They obeyed. Even Mamma stepped back.

Rosa dipped the brush and carefully wiped the excess ink on the rim of the pot. She took a deep breath, which was echoed through the kitchen and held, as she put the brush down on the white pasteboard and began to form the first words, the lettering so clean that even Miss Finch would have been forced to admire it.

WE WANT BREAD, she wrote on the first line. Everyone who could read English nodded and murmured the words to the others. Yes, yes, of course they wanted bread.

AND ROSES TOO

Mamma gave a little gasp. But Rosa was not finished. One more dip and she put a perfectly curved comma between *ROSES* and *TOO*—in case, just in case, Miss Finch were to see the sign and marvel that these ignorant foreigners should know enough to insert a comma. Careful not to drip, she replaced the brush in the pot.

Meantime, Anna was reading the second line aloud and then the whole sign. Something like a little cheer went up, and everyone leaned in for a closer look at the masterpiece.

"No, no!" Mrs. Marino yelled, spreading her arms out once again. "It'sa still wet. Don'ta touch, nobody! It'sa *bellissimo!* Ooh, Rosa, *bambina mia!* It'sa the best sign nobody ever made!" She took Rosa's head in both her big red hands and kissed the part in her hair. She was weeping for joy.

There were tears in Mamma's eyes as well. "Don' I say she's top of class?"

After Mrs. Marino pronounced the lettering completely dry, Anna carefully nailed the pasteboard to a broken broomstick, and the ladies went home to cut the bread for their families' meager noon meal. When they gathered later to march to the station, Mrs. Marino asked Rosa if she wanted to carry her sign. It was then she remembered all over again that she wanted no part of this strike—this strike for which she had just that morning made the "best sign nobody ever made." "No," she said. "It's Mamma's sign. It was all her idea. She should carry it."

"You sure?" Mamma asked, the excitement of carrying the wonderful sign already sparkling in her dark eyes.

"I'm sure," Rosa said. "I'm not really part of the strike. I'm not a worker. I shouldn't be in the parade."

There was a murmur of disagreement from the women. Hadn't she just made the best sign, the *bellissimo* best sign? But they were eager to be off with their beautiful sign, which was sure to get the attention of Mr. Big Bill Haywood, who was coming all the way from the miners' strike far out west to support them, the foreign mill workers of Lawrence, Massachusetts.

At the door, Mamma saw that Rosa was hanging back. "Come along, Rosina, it's going to be great parade. Thousand, thousand marchers. Mr. Big Bill Haywood come all a way cross America just for us. You don' wanta miss it, eh?"

"I got homework," Rosa said. But it wasn't homework, it was the knot in her stomach, which never seemed to loosen, that kept her from witnessing what the local newspaper later called "the greatest demonstration ever accorded a visitor in Lawrence." There were more than 15,000 people at the station to greet Mr. Big Bill Haywood and the famous woman organizer, Mrs. Elizabeth Gurley Flynn, but Rosa was not among them. She was on her bed at home, praying to the Virgin to keep her mamma and sister safe. The sign would be noticed, she was sure of that, but how could it be good to be noticed when you were up against the powerful Mr. Billy Wood and the mayor and the police and the militia and the governor—the whole state of Massachusetts, maybe even the whole United States of America? And if Mamma got put in jail—or hurt—or killed—whose fault would it be then? She had made the best sign. It would be on her head. She slid under the quilt and pulled it over her guilty head, although it was still daylight outside the tenement door.

Nine

The Beautiful
Mrs. Gurley Flynn

JAKE WAS WOUND up tighter than string on a top. So wound up after a week of stealing food and sleeping in garbage heaps that, without meaning to, he let himself get caught up in the excitement of Sunday's mob. There were thousands of them, all pressing toward the train station. Someone was coming to town. Someone, judging from the feverish pitch of the crowd, who they believed was going to settle things for them once and for all.

Jake was shorter than the men crowded about him, and he could see nothing except the dirty coat of the man whose body he was shoved against. But Jake was thin as an empty spool and quite used to weaseling his way through crowded streets, so by the time he heard the whistle and then the powerful chugging of the great locomotive, he was in the front row of spectators.

The train stopped with a squeal of brakes and a great whoosh of steam. The crowd roared, and people began to jostle one another for a better view. Flags and signs were raised high above the heads of those carrying them. If Jake had been able to read, he might have known whose name was painted on them, who was of such almighty importance that this enormous crowd had braved the cold and the threats of the authorities to meet his train at the station. Then, as though to answer his question, the crowd began a chant, "Big Bill! Big Bill!"

The brakes had hardly stopped squealing when a huge man in a cowboy hat leaped off the train, not even waiting for the porter to set the steps beside the car. His eyes swept the crowd. One of his eyes was milky white, which made him look like a fierce half-blind giant. It gave Jake a shiver, but no one else seemed daunted. They screamed their welcome. The man waved his big hat and smiled. Coming down the steps behind him was a small group of men and, of all things, a young woman. The other men couldn't hold a candle to the one who must be the "Big Bill" the crowd had shouted for, but the woman . . . the woman simply took Jake's breath away. She wore a large soft hat that almost hid what seemed to be a mound of black hair. Her skin was creamy white, her waist narrower than Big Bill's neck, her eyes clear and blue as a summer sky. Jake put his hand on his chest to keep his heart from jumping right out of his shirt. He couldn't stop staring at her. She was enough to make anyone want to join their blasted union.

Her eyes flashed with excitement as one of the three

bands struck up a tune. The Syrian band wasn't here to greet the newcomers. Jake knew from the talk on the street that their leader was in jail for hiding dynamite. Ha! Did those fool bosses think *anyone* was going to believe that some little Syrian shopkeeper was going to risk his life to dynamite a mill? Jake spit his contempt toward the dirty snow but hit the shoes of the marcher beside him instead. Fortunately, the man was cheering so vigorously he hadn't noticed.

The three bands took turns playing tunes, and at the end of each song a different part of the crowd roared approval—some tune from their old country, Jake guessed. Then all three bands together began to play tunes that made the police and militia tighten their grips on their guns and glare nervously at the marchers.

"Hey, Jake boy! Where you been?" It was Angelo and his housemates, including Giuliano, who was probably still mad about his ruined shirt. Well, Jake couldn't help ruining the man's shirt, could he? He hadn't asked his pa to beat him bloody, now, had he? Just then, the crowd turned to escort Big Bill and his party to the common, and Jake was able to avoid his one-time companions. But it was stupid of him, wasn't it? Angelo had seemed glad to see him. Jake could probably sleep in their place and eat regularly if he caught up with them. After all, he hadn't stolen anything from *their* apartment—just bloodied grumpy little Giuliano's shirt.

The party from the train and the leaders of the strike from Lawrence, now including Ettor and Giovannitti, both of whom the workers had embraced as their own, began to make their way through the crowd toward the common. They passed so close to Jake that he could have reached out and touched the beautiful woman, but he didn't quite dare. He let the crowd turn him around so as to follow the leaders. The crowd joined the bands, singing raucously along, seemingly oblivious of the police and militia lining the route. It took a long time for the thousands to walk the five blocks from the station to the common—time to sing plenty of songs before everyone was assembled in front of the makeshift platform on which *she* stood, shining like a star among the dark-coated men.

The speeches finally began. Jake wasn't much for speeches, but he waited, hoping she would speak. One good thing about crowds like this—everyone was packed so tightly together that the only thing that could get cold was his feet. There was no way to keep them out of the icy slush. Even though he was impatient for the men to shut up and let the lady speak, he had to admit that Big Bill was impressive—his voice was so powerful, he probably could have been heard all the way to Canal Street.

"I have read in the newspapers," the big man said, "that Lawrence was afraid of me. It is not the people of Lawrence who are fearful; it is the superintendents, agents, and owners of the mills." The crowd roared. Then he gazed over their heads at the militia lining the streets around the common. "I have been in strikes where soldiers were at hand," he told the crowd, "but I never saw a strike defeated by soldiers."

Jake joined in the cries of approval, but his eyes were not on Big Bill; they were on the woman at Big Bill's side. He couldn't keep his eyes off her. Just looking at her made a flame start at his frozen toes and shoot through his body all the way to the hairs on his head. Then and there he determined to join the strike activity, just so he could follow her around.

The next day, Jake found out that she would be speaking to the women strikers in the Franco-Belgian Hall. He didn't care that it was a women's meeting where only women and children would be welcome. He forgot that a few days earlier he had been proud when that silly schoolboy Joe O'Brien had taken him for a man. If he had to turn into a kid to get into a meeting where his goddess was speaking, he'd be a kid.

She saw him staring up at her as she was being introduced, or he guessed that it was an introduction. It was all in French. She looked him in the face and smiled . . . *smiled* right at him, Jake Beale. He felt faint and was too befuddled to smile back. At last, she began to speak. To his delight, she spoke in English and then waited patiently while one of the women strikers turned it into French. She would have to leave Lawrence right away, she said. The women protested. "I don't want to leave you," she explained, "but I have to go and collect money from other chapters of our union. This may be a long strike, and your brother and sister members of the Industrial Workers of the World will want to support you. You must have food for yourselves and your children. You must have money to buy fuel for your stoves in this cold weather. Your job is to stand together, to oppose all who would weaken your resolve—to march, to picket. My job is to gather the funds to support your cause." She smiled at them all. "But I will be back, I promise."

There was no point in going to meetings if she wasn't going to be there. Without her presence, all the light was gone from those gloomy halls. For the rest of the week, Jake went back to spending nights in garbage piles and stealing food, and he went to the various halls only when he knew there would be soup. While there, he always kept his mouth shut so no one would guess he was native-born and not one of the immigrant strikers. The one time he dared go to the Italian hall, he thought he saw the shoe girl ahead of him in line. He left quickly, before she could see him, though why should he avoid her? Hadn't he left good money—a whole penny— behind the last time he slept in her kitchen? Sometimes he didn't understand himself.

By Friday it seemed to him that Mrs. Gurley Flynn, as he now knew she was called, had forgotten her promise, that she would never return. He was tired and bored and wretched. Why not go back to work and earn some money? The bosses were paying the scabs good wages. So he started for work that morning, only to be stopped two blocks above Canal Street by a huge woman who screamed threats in his face in Italian, ending with a large hand soundly slapping his bottom and a command in English: "No scab! Go home!"

Somehow he was more afraid of these big women than he was of the police on their horses or the little tin-soldier militia with their guns and bayonets.

All that day, as he walked wearily around the town, he heard the rumor that Joe Ettor had gone to Boston to meet Billy Wood and demand a fifteen percent pay raise for all the workers. Hah! Not that Jake could figure what fifteen percent of five dollars and twenty-five cents would amount to—but why should it matter? He might not be able to do much figuring, but he could figure well enough to know that Billy Wood was not going to add a penny to his wages.

By Sunday he was so cold and tired that he went to every Mass in Holy Rosary Church just so he could get some sleep. He was too tired to trot up to the altar with the hope of getting one of those little paper crackers, but he could doze through the Latin gibberish. He would have stayed longer, except that one of those Italian papists must have spotted him. At any rate, the priest came down the aisle after the church had emptied following the noon Mass and asked him what he was doing sleeping through three Masses in a row. Jake hurried out, giving a backward glance at the poor box. The lock looked flimsy enough to warrant a return visit.

🌷 Ten

Anarchy

THE SCANT DOZEN CHILDREN LEFT in Rosa's class sat at their desks, puzzled into silence. The bell had rung some time ago, and still no Miss Finch. There was an almost sepulchral solemnity about her absence. Teachers, in the students' experience, were always in the classroom. They had no life outside that room. Therefore, they were never tardy, much less absent. Tardiness, to hear Miss Finch expound on the subject, was one of the seven deadly sins.

Then how to account for the missing Miss Finch? What should they do?

At length, Rosa opened her single textbook, her history book, and tried to reread the dense description of the Constitutional Convention. Out of the corner of her eye she could see that the Khoury boys had put their heads down on their desks to get a head start on their morning naps. Celina Cosa had unbraided both of her pigtails and was carefully rebraiding one.

Celina caught Rosa looking. "She's dead," Celina said. Someone several rows back let out a snort. Celina whipped about. "It ain't funny. She'll go straight to hell, being a Protestant and all."

Rosa was shocked. Of course, she knew the church taught that if you weren't Catholic you were lost, but she'd never actually applied it to people she knew. Certainly not to Miss Finch, who was so proper—who was always here, never tardy, and was, in her prim, old-maidish way, trying desperately to turn them into good, clean, educated American citizens.

She was even more shocked when, a few minutes later, Miss Finch came bursting through the door, her hat askew, her hair flying loose from her always perfect bun, her coat half buttoned.

She was panting like a stray dog. "They attacked my trolley car!" she cried. "They threw rocks at us. I was only trying to get to school!" She paused to catch her breath. "Oh, children, didn't I warn you there would be terrible violence? These Marxist agitators are turning your people into animals . . . *animals!* I barely escaped with my life, and then I had to run—I had to run all the way to get here to you." She plopped down on her chair, exhausted.

The children sat riveted, staring at her as she sought to pull herself together. "It began with snowballs and ice. Now . . ." She looked down at her coat and began, with shaking fingers, to undo the remaining buttons. Then she stood, slipped off her coat, and laid it on her desk. They watched her, as entranced as though they were attending a performance. She reached up and took the pins out of her hat, removed it, returned the pins to the crown of the hat, and set it on top of the overcoat. Then she felt her hair. Abruptly, she picked up the hat and coat and started for the cloakroom at the rear of the class-room. The class sat in stunned silence and waited for her to re-emerge, her hair now pinned into its usual tight bun, her face looking remarkably calmer.

"Celina," she said, "this is not your boudoir, my dear. Kindly go to the cloakroom to finish dressing your hair." Celina rose to her feet, still clutching her half-braided hank of hair. She kept her head turned to watch the teacher and tripped over her shoes as she made her way to the back of the room.

"Now, children, don't be afraid. I'm sure you're as upset as I am that this strike has turned so ugly. I've tried so hard to warn you what might happen. Your parents are being led astray by these anarchists and Marxists. I'm not sure we've discussed Marxism yet. Suffice it to say, all Marxists are atheists. That means, they do not believe in God. We have talked, I know, about anarchism." She looked down into Rosa's face. "Can you tell the class what an anarchist is, Rosa?"

"It's—they're people who don't trust the government."

"Yes, but it's more than that, isn't it?" The teacher's

voice was kind. She wanted so much for them to understand. "Anarchists not only mistrust government, they want to be rid of the government. They're lawless, and they're proud of being lawless. And what," she stopped to look at each of the children in turn, "what would life be like if there were no laws? No policemen to protect us from those who would harm us?"

"A policeman beat up my mama."

Rosa did not have the nerve to turn and see whose quiet voice had dared challenge the teacher.

"I'm sure the policeman was only trying to help keep order," Miss Finch said. "It's very hard for them, you know, when thousands of people are threatening them every day. Preparing to dynamite the mills, throwing rocks—"

"The workers didn't set no dynamite, Miss Finch. That was a trick."

Now Rosa did turn to see who had the gall to take up Joe O'Brien's role as teacher's challenger, which had disappeared when he was arrested. She was startled to realize that it was tiny Olga Kronsky, who had hardly ever spoken out in class in her life, which was why Rosa hadn't recognized her voice. "My mama said the owners'd do anything to make the strikers look bad. Maybe those Pinkerton men they hired was the very ones who threw them rocks at your trolley car. Joe Ettor said if anything bad happened, they'd always try to make it look like the workers done it."

"Did it. The workers did it, Olga."

"No, ma'am, they ain't done nothing."

"They *haven't done anything,* Olga, not *they ain't done nothing.*"

"But that's what I mean, Miss Finch, my mama ain't done nothing. Joe Ettor said, 'No violence,' and that's what we done. We ain't done no violence."

Rosa could tell from the look on Olga's face that she had no idea it was her grammar and not her protest that Miss Finch was trying to amend. Miss Finch apparently realized that her cause was hopeless. She sighed deeply and sat down at her desk. "Very well, Olga. I'm afraid you'll be disillusioned soon enough. Ah, welcome back, Celina, you look very nice now."

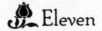 Eleven

The Day Hell Breaks Loose

J AKE WAS SICK OF IT ALL—the grubbing for food, the
nasty places where he had to sleep or the churches
where he tried to sleep but which didn't welcome strays
like him, who came only for shelter from the winter wind
and a chance to pilfer pennies. There had been those few
moments with Angelo, and then again when he saw Mrs.
Gurley Flynn, when he had almost thought the strike
was a good thing, but the feeling hadn't lasted. He had
no national hall to march proudly into for warmth and
food and companionship during these dark days. There
was nothing in the strike for the likes of him but cold
and hunger.

So on that Monday, more than two weeks after the
infernal business had begun, he determined once again
to return to work. He would earn the money to buy his
pa enough whiskey to keep him from beating him, and
go back and live in the shack by the river that he had
called home since he could remember. He remembered

quite well how much he had hated that old life, but this new one was worse. He never knew what to expect from day to day. And he was so cold. He would save out from his pay envelope at least enough money to buy coal for the shack's little stove. Yes, he'd make a fire at night and sleep close to it.

The crowds on Canal Street were almost as thick as they had been at the station the week before. But they were angry, booing and yelling at workers who were trying to elbow their way through to get to the mill gates or over the canal bridge and on to the Wood or Ayer mills. "Scab! Scab!" they screamed, along with what he guessed were obscenities in their native tongues. He persisted and was nearly at the bridge when a rough hand grabbed his arm.

"You ain't scabbing, is you, boy?" It was Giuliano.

Jake decided on the spot that he'd have to give up trying to get to work that day. "No, no," he said. "I come to help picket."

"I better not catch you crossing that bridge!"

"I wouldn't!" Jake answered, wriggling out of Giuliano's grasp. "Scab! Scab!" he yelled as he moved away from the angry man . . . and right into the legs of a giant horse. The policeman astride it reached down and whacked him on the shoulder with a club. Jake cried out in surprise and then cursed the officer in the one language he was sure to understand.

"Why, you foul-mouthed little devil!" The policeman pulled his horse back and used its great flank to push Jake toward the canal.

Hell's bells! He means to drive me right into the water! The canal water was so filthy that if you didn't freeze to death, the poison would kill you for sure. Jake dodged away, edging toward a man with a huge American flag, who was yelling at the crowd to follow him up Union Street. People were coming from picket lines farther east on Canal and joining the crowd. Somebody started to sing. Not having gone to many meetings, Jake didn't know any of the songs, but he liked the sound of them and it calmed his anger a little to listen.

The whole mood of the strikers seemed to lighten on the walk up the hill. It felt more like the crowd that had greeted Big Bill and Mrs. Gurley Flynn. Maybe she'd come back after all. Hadn't she promised she would, bringing money and help for the strikers? His own heart warmed as he remembered her, standing in front of the foreign women as if she wasn't any better than they were—as though they were sisters or something. The marchers were just passing the Everett Mill when, above the singing, he heard a shot. Everyone heard it, for the music stopped abruptly and the crowd froze.

Some looked toward the mill to see where the shot might have come from; others looked toward the police and militia lining the route. Jake didn't bother to investigate. If there was shooting, he just wanted to get away. As he began to wriggle his way through the stunned marchers, he could hear the murmurs passing from mouth to mouth.

"They killed her!"

"She's dead."

"Annie Lopizzo . . . You know the girl. She work at the Everett."

"No, no, she work at Pacific."

But what did it matter where she had worked if she was dead?

He made his way to the Polish bakery—the place where the clerk had given him coffee and a bun after that terrible night when Pa had beat him bloody. He didn't care if they remembered him or not. He wanted to be safe and warm and to have something in his stomach. Then maybe he could decide what to do next.

The door was open, and a bell rang. The girl he had seen before came into the shop from the bakery in the back. "Can I help you?" she asked. She didn't seem to recognize him.

"They shot someone," he said.

"Who, who shot—?"

"The police. We was just marching peaceful-like up Union, and just before we got to Garden. . . ."

"Did you see it?" Her eyes were wide; she was clearly frightened.

"Oh, yeah. She didn't do nothing, and they just shot her dead."

"They shot a *woman?*" The girl sat down on a stool, stunned.

He nodded, having no idea how old the person had been.

"And I was thinking things would be better now."

"Better?"

"You didn't hear? They found out who hid the dynamite. And it wasn't any worker."

He was more interested in the tray of buns behind the glass, but he knew better than to seem so. "Then who done it?"

"Breen. You know—the Irish undertaker. His pa was mayor once."

"Why would *he* do such a fool thing?"

"Because he's a fool. He wrapped the sticks in a copy of his own undertakers' journal before he hid them. He was even the one tipped off the police where to look for them." She shook her head in disbelief. "Whoever paid him ought to get a refund." She sighed and got up. "But you come in for something more than the news."

He bit his lip.

"It's okay. Nobody's got money. Would you like a raisin bun, boy?"

He nodded. She reached in and chose a large one. Then another. "Here. Take two. We'll be closing soon, especially if things get wild out there. They won't be fresh tomorrow."

Jake went back out into the noisy street, chewing the sweet doughy bread, the second bun tucked under his shirt for later. It had begun to snow heavily and was likely to turn into a brute of a storm before morning. He waited until dark, then slipped into Holy Rosary, broke open the poor box, and, for his troubles, got two pennies. He knew better than to sleep in the church he'd just robbed and headed through the blowing snow for Saint Mary's. He'd just have to avoid the Irish sexton.

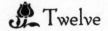 Twelve

Who Killed Annie Lopizzo?

"I DON' WANT YOU to go to school today, Rosa."

Rosa nodded, relieved. She didn't want to go to school today, either. The colonel of the militia, blaming Annie Lopizzo's death on the strikers, said his men were to "shoot to kill." Wasn't it in the paper? Anyhow, everyone knew he'd said it. "We are not looking for peace now!" Colonel Sweetser had added, just in case the strikers misunderstood. Who would want to be on the street after hearing that? Rosa hardly wanted to get out of bed.

But she knew Mamma meant that she was to stay home to help prepare for the funeral. Although Mamma and Anna hardly knew Annie Lopizzo, she had been one of them, one of their sister strikers, and the women of the neighborhood were determined that the mourners at her funeral outnumber even the crowd that had greeted Big Bill.

It had all seemed so hopeful then. *We want bread and roses, too.* All week they had been glowing with pride and determination. But just as things seemed to be getting better, the bottom of their world had dropped out. Annie Lopizzo was dead and not yet in the grave before they learned that mild, little Mr. Caruso had been jailed for the killing, and that Joe Ettor and Arturo Giovannitti, who weren't anywhere near Union and Garden streets at the time, had been accused of inciting the violence and had therefore been arrested as accessories. So their two leaders were now in jail for murder as well. And that same terrible day, the Syrian boy who had been bayoneted two weeks earlier had died from his wounds.

"And they dare call *us* violent!" Mamma cried to the women assembled in the kitchen.

"Beautiful Signor Giovannitti! He will die in the prison! A poet is like a wild and lovely bird, yes? You cage him and he cannota sing, so he die!" Mrs. Marino put her apron over her head and began to weep.

"But what we do widout Mr. Ettor and Mr. Giovannitti to lead us?" Mrs. Petrovsky asked the question in all their hearts. "What we do now?"

"We do just what we do before. We march, we sing, we never, never, *never* give in," said Mamma.

And she wouldn't, Rosa knew, and she saw Mamma lying in the street in a pool of her own red blood. Holy Mary, how could Rosa keep her home? A huge funeral with thousands of mourners would invite bloodshed. "Shoot to kill!" the colonel had said. From jail Joe Ettor sent word that all must stay calm, for the only peace the authorities wanted was the peace of the cemetery.

"Come, Rosina, we go pay our respect."

"I don't feel well," Rosa said.

"Sick or well, we all go. Even Ricci. Annie Lopizzo is my sister."

So . . . they would all die. It was as simple as that. Mamma was determined. The dread was so heavy that Rosa felt the weight of it, as though she was carrying a sack of coal on her back. But the fear had numbed to resignation. How, after all, could she live if Mamma, Anna, and Ricci were dead? She might as well die with them.

The body was laid out in the DeCesare funeral parlor on Common Street. It was the same place Papa had been taken after the fire at the mill. She thought she might throw up on the snow as they approached it. There had been a blizzard the night Annie had died. "God himself is fury," Mamma had said. So now they stood ankle deep in freezing slush outside the undertaker's. There was no singing, hardly any talking, as the long line of strikers waited patiently to be allowed in to the viewing. The only voices were the shouts of the militia as they surrounded the crowd and yelled down orders and threats from horseback. No one in the crowd seemed to be paying them any attention; they stood quietly, not so much out of fear of the threats as out of respect for the dead.

To Rosa's amazement, their turn finally came. They entered the parlor, where the casket sat on a bier. Someone must have paid. It was so much nicer than Papa's casket, and even though it was January, there were flowers, including a huge display with a ribbon: FROM THE POLISH WORKERS TO THE VICTIM OF CAPITALISM. They passed by the body. Mamma leaned over and kissed the corpse, just as though Annie Lopizzo had really been her blood kin. It took only a few minutes, and then they were out in the cold air again and walking home. As they climbed the stairs to the apartment, the dread rolled off Rosa's back. She remembered the story in a strange Protestant book she'd sneaked a look at in the library. It told of a man carrying a huge burden marked "Sin," which at the foot of the cross simply slid off his back and rolled away. But her relief didn't last much past the front door. Mamma was already talking about going to the funeral the next day.

"Listen to this, Mamma," Anna was saying. "They were passing this around at the funeral parlor. It's another message from Joe Ettor."

"What does our Mr. Joe Ettor say?"

"He says: 'Tomorrow will be the funeral of our sister who was dreaming the same dreams and aspiring to the same hopes to which you aspire—'"

Mamma interrupted. "What mean 'aspire'?" They both looked at Rosa.

"I don't know . . . maybe, the hopes you want to happen. Something like that."

Anna went on. ". . . 'aspiring to the same hopes to which you aspire, but she is one of the victims of the struggle. . . . We will gather and escort our fellow worker to her last resting place. We meet to pay our last sad tribute to our comrade who has parted with her life blood in the struggle."

"He can't meet anybody," Rosa protested. "He's in jail."

"He has big spirit," Mamma said. "His spirit meet alla time with us."

The Jarusalises came in noisily and put a welcome end to the conversation. Mamma made Anna read the message again, interrupting only to say, "Aspire mean want for to happen, eh, Rosa?"

"Goot message," Mrs. Jarusalis pronounced and turned to interpret it for Granny. Then the women and girls fell to exchanging plans for gathering the next day. There must be a huge crowd to follow the hearse.

"Bigger than crowd that meet Mr. Big Bill Haywood," Mamma said again, and they all agreed.

Rosa slipped out of the kitchen to take refuge in the bedroom. Jonas and Kestutis were already asleep on their cot, and Granny was putting Ricci to bed in the back room. Rosa put on Papa's old shirt that she used for a winter nightgown and got under the quilt. No one had spoken of supper, so she must conclude that there was none to be had tonight. Before long, Mamma and Mrs. J. and the girls were going through the room—on their way to their halls to get orders for the next day, she was sure. She pretended to be asleep. She was so tired, her bones ached.

She was still tossing sleeplessly when the four of them returned. "But Colonel Sweetser *promised* Joe Ettor we could march to the cemetery!" Anna was saying as they came through the door, oblivious of the fact that Granny and the boys were asleep and Rosa was pretending to be.

"Promises! Promises!" Mamma said. "Promises don' mean nothing to such. He say we be violent. I say, 'Who be violent?' You stab dead Syrian boy. You shoot dead our sister! Who be the violent ones, eh?"

Next morning the kitchen meeting began before dawn. The pronouncement had come down: Only one car would be allowed to follow the horse-drawn hearse. No marchers. Only the single car, carrying Annie Lopizzo's one living relative and a friend or two—that was it. The mood of the women gathered in the Serutti kitchen was bleaker than the winter sky outside. Their leaders were in jail, and Colonel Sweetser's men had made it deadly clear that they meant to follow his orders. They would shoot to kill, and any resulting deaths would be blamed on the strikers, who would, no doubt, hang for the crime.

"I got me a good kitchen knife—long asa my arm," Mrs. Marino muttered.

"No, no." Mamma laid her hand down on her friend's arm, as though afraid the knife were there already. "No violence. Mr. Joe Ettor say, 'No violence.'"

"Then they shoot us, every one."

"No, no, we keep together. Solidarity. Remember, Mrs. Marino. Solidarity, and no matter what, we win."

"No matter if we dead, who gonna win." Mrs. Marino was shaking her head. "They——" She stabbed the table with her fist. "They poke their bayonet into boy, never have a beard. They shoot young girl, never have chance to marry, have children. Who they don't kill now? *Dio mio,* don't they have no heart?"

Rosa, standing against the open bedroom door, was trembling so hard she put out one hand to steady herself on the frame. Mrs. Marino was right. Who wouldn't they shoot or stab? That day she'd followed Mamma to the march, she had seen the fear in the Harvard boys' eyes— like stray dogs cornered in an alley. They'd attack if they felt threatened. And they would blame the strikers. The lucky ones, like Joe O'Brien's snowballers, might go to jail for a year—the rest, like Joe Ettor, were likely to be hanged.

How could Mamma believe for one minute that the strikers could win? Maybe, as Mamma claimed, they didn't plant the dynamite or attack the trolleys, but they would soon. They were cornered and desperate, too. Already black hands had appeared on the doors of scabbing workers. You didn't have to be Italian to know the meaning of a black hand painted on your door. Why, even here in their own home, there was talk of kitchen knives.

Anxiously, she scanned the faces in the room. The women weren't all close neighbors. They weren't even all Italian. Suppose—the thought chilled her—just suppose there were a spy among them? Joe Ettor and Mr. Giovannitti were in jail for murder, but they hadn't even been near Garden and Union and the two of them were always pleading, "No violence." What of women who talked openly of kitchen knives as long as their arms? What of a woman in whose kitchen such words had been spoken? *Oh, Mamma, Mamma, don't be such a fool. There is no winning. Only death.* Her heart was pounding so hard against her ribs that she was in pain from it.

"Anna, Marija," Mamma was saying. "Go to Chabis Hall. See if there is soup tonight. We need our strength, eh?"

Had Mamma forgotten there were troops all over everywhere, with orders to shoot to kill? Was she out of her mind? Rosa couldn't help herself. "No!" The word came out in a squeak. "Mamma, no! Don't make them go to the hall. They'll get killed!"

"Oh, Rosina," Mamma said. "They big girls. They

know how to behave." And Anna and Marija were gone almost before she had finished the sentence.

Mamma came over to where Rosa stood crying by the door. She put her arms around Rosa's shaking body, "Shh, shh." She began rubbing Rosa's back, murmuring to her so low that the women around the kitchen table couldn't hear her. "Shh, shh. Don' be so 'fraid, *bambina*. I don' send your sister out to die. I send her to find can we eat tonight. Soldier, or no soldier, we gotta eat, eh? Is there bread in this house? I don' see none. Do you? So what we do? Sit like scared rabbit in our kitchen and shake and starve? We can't do that, eh? Now, go wash your face and read your book or something. We be all right, you see."

Rosa went to the toilet in the hall. It stank to high heaven, but it was the only private place in her world. She sat down on the seat without pulling up her dress and let out the sobs that had been building up ever since the first riot alarms had rung. It seemed like years. It was hardly three weeks. But it would go on forever. She would always be hungry and cold and afraid. She was sure of it.

She was back in the front room lying on her bed when she heard the big girls rattling up the staircase outside. They burst through her door and ran into the kitchen without even stopping to close the door behind them. "They're coming, Mamma, they're coming!"

"Who?"

"What she say?"

All the women in the kitchen were on their feet, crowding around the girls for the news.

Rosa got up to close the door, one ear toward the other room. Despite everything, she had to hear what had happened.

"Mrs. Gurley Flynn and Big Bill! They're coming back. The strike committee wants them to lead the strike while Joe Ettor's in jail."

"Santa Maria! Grazie, grazie."

The strike would go on. The union was making sure that it would. And how many more would die?

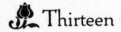 Thirteen

An Unexpected Bath

S HE WAS COMING BACK! Mrs. Gurley Flynn and the one they called Big Bill were coming back to Lawrence to lead the strike. The most beautiful woman in the world was coming back to help them . . . to help *him*. Wasn't he on strike against Mr. Billy Wood as much as anybody? Well, he hadn't scabbed, had he? No matter how cold and hungry he was, he, Jake Beale, had never once crossed that cursed bridge and gone through those iron gates.

Jake brushed aside the times he had been on the verge of crossing the bridge and heading back into the mill. He hadn't, though, had he? Something or someone had always stopped him. God or fate or furious little Giuliano. He wouldn't have to feel ashamed when he saw her again. He could hold his head high. He was one of the oppressed workers she was coming to save.

There was soup in the halls these days after Annie Lopizzo's death. It had got them a lot of sympathy. In the halls where he sneaked in to eat, in the shops, on the streets, people talked about how, in the rest of the entire U.S. of A., everyone knew how the law in Lawrence was twisted to suit the mill owners. That fool Breen laying that dynamite—and who had paid him? Not the strikers, that was for sure. The girl in the Polish bakery told Jake that the stupid man had no more sense than to wrap the sticks in copies of his undertakers' journal, with his own name on the address label—not likely that a striker would have copies of that lying around.

"But now undertaker Breen is out on bail while the men who threw snowballs are in jail until next year. And what, what will become of Mr. Ettor and Mr. Giovannitti, who had nothing to do with Annie Lopizzo's death? They'll probably hang."

Jake listened, trying hard to look properly sorrowful, but all he could think about was that Mrs. Gurley Flynn was coming back. She would know the truth behind all the government lies. She'd make them own up to all their plots and wickedness. He had to see her. Since Ettor and Giovannitti's arrest, meetings on the common had been outlawed. The only places left to meet were the national halls. She mostly went where the women and children gathered, but, by golly, he'd be a kid—or even a woman—Italian, Polish, Turk, whatever it took to weasel his way into every meeting where she was to speak. He might even get himself a bit of grub while he was at it.

Maybe she would notice him again. Not merely smile this time but pick him out special-like, tell him how brave he was—just a boy, too—to stand up to the owners, to suffer hunger and cold and homelessness, so that he could go on being a part of this great strike.

He snuffled. His nose was always running these days. As he wiped it on the back of his sleeve, he saw to his horror how dirty his shirt was. If his clothes were that filthy, what of his face? He'd never bothered about bathing before—didn't really believe in it. But she was so clean, so white and lovely, her cheeks like roses on fresh snow. What would she think of a boy like him?

For the first time in his life, he needed to know what his face looked like. The only mirror he knew of was in the sacristy of Saint Mary's. There was also running water in there, in case he decided to wash up a bit. He wasn't about to wash in the canal. Not only was it frozen and smelly, everyone knew it would make you sick to death if you got a drop or two in your mouth. There was nothing for it. He'd have to go into Saint Mary's and hide out somewhere inside until after dark.

He went to noon Mass. Well, it was warm in there, and nobody paid attention to him. He slid under the pew afterward so the sexton wouldn't see him as he came down the aisle, checking for trash. Without meaning to, he fell fast asleep. He hadn't had a decent night's sleep since he could remember, and the church, though drafty, seemed almost toasty compared with a trash heap. When he woke up, it was pitch dark except for the little light on the altar and the tiny candles—not so many lit now that people had no money. He felt his way down the aisle and up on the platform. It was like being a blind man, and he wouldn't have minded, but he had the urge and he wanted to get into that priests' secret little toilet as fast as he could. He found the door, fumbled at the knob, and opened it. There was an electric bulb hanging from the ceiling and he managed to find the chain and pull it, which gave him ample light to find the privy.

The basin had a mirror over it, so after he had relieved himself, he went to study his face in the shadowy light. His eyes were the thing that struck him. He leaned close to the mirror. They were blue, surrounded by whites that were blood streaked. His face was dark as a Spaniard's—but that was probably the dirt. He ran water into the basin. There was a towel hanging nearby, so he wet it and began methodically to wipe his face. Eventually, it came a lighter shade, but still, in the shadowy light, it seemed to him that he looked as gray and tired as an old man. Why would someone so beautiful lower herself to talk to the likes of him? He didn't want her pity—though with a face like that he might get her pity—he wanted her to like him, to think he was somebody good and brave, somebody on the way to becoming a hero like Joe Ettor or Big Bill. With this face, she was likely to see him as just some bum kid, somebody who slept in trash piles and pilfered poor boxes. Of course, he knew that that was what he was, but he had to be, didn't he? Had the world given him any choice? Well, it was going to be different from now on. He'd stick with the strikers, eat at the halls when there was food, and find someplace decent to sleep—maybe at Angelo's or at the shoe girl's.

He grabbed some of the paper crackers from the cabinet, took a swig, just a small one, from the priests' supply of wine, turned off the light, and went back into the dark sanctuary. As he felt his way across the altar toward where he thought the stairs must be, his foot hit something, something soft. He gave a little squeak of surprise. At the same time, the lump he'd tripped against rose up from its knees and grabbed his shirt. He was pulled right off his feet until his face was next to a much larger face, so close that when the man spoke, the spit from his mouth hit Jake's carefully wiped cheek.

"What are you doing in the sacristy, you little thief?"

Jake's feelings were hurt. How could it be stealing to take a little water, a few crackers, and a small, very small, swig of wine? "Nothing," he said. "I ain't no thief."

"Mercy, boy, you smell like a canal rat." The hand put Jake's feet to the floor but held tightly to his shirt.

"Don't," Jake said. "You'll rip me shirt."

The hand moved to take his arm. "Come with me,

son." If there had been any choice, Jake would have hightailed it out of there, but wriggle as he did, he could not break the steel grip on his arm.

He was dragged out a side door, across an alley, and into another building, where there was enough light for him to see that his captor was none other than Father James O'Reilly, who was head of Saint Mary's and, by rumor, the real boss of every other Catholic church in town.

"Mrs. O'Sullivan!" his captor roared. A small woman came scurrying from somewhere, wiping her hands on a large apron as she ran.

"Yes, Father?"

"Take this little heathen and clean him up for me, will you?"

"But I'm in the way of fixing your dinner, Father."

"Dinner can wait. Put him in the tub and scrub him within an inch of his life."

"But, Father," the woman was turning quite red, "he's not a baby. He's a growing boy. It don't seem proper—"

"Oh, woman, get Father Donahue, then. He's got to be cleaned. Can't you smell him from there?"

"But why, Father? Surely, he has a home and parents who—"

"I very much doubt that they, if they exist, have ever bathed him, and I won't have anyone eating in my kitchen who smells worse than the rubbish outside the door."

☙ ☙ ☙

Jake's first impulse was to struggle, but the warm water in the tub was surprisingly soothing, so he just sat there and let the young priest scrub away. His back was still sore, and when the priest's hand reached toward it, he winced. The priest shook his head at the sight of the welts and was very gentle there. Even Jake's hair was doused with water and scrubbed with the strong yellow soap. The water in which he sat was almost as black as the water in the canal, and before he was done, the priest let it all out and drew clean water to rinse off the soap. He dried Jake with a large towel and then wrapped the towel around him.

"Now," the young priest said, "don't you feel better?"

Strange was more like it. He felt strange, as though he were no longer himself, that the yellow soap had scraped Jake Beale clean away and revealed someone else, someone he'd never met before.

The priest left the room. Jake would have escaped at that point, but his clothes had disappeared and he didn't fancy going out into the winter evening with nothing but a towel wrapped around him. And besides, hadn't O'Reilly said something about supper? In a few minutes, the young priest returned, bringing with him a pair of trousers and a shirt.

"They're not new, but better than what you had, I dare say." He turned his back to let Jake put on the clothes. The cuffs of the shirt were a bit frayed, but Jake had to roll them up anyway. He folded the pant legs a turn or two as well.

"I'm sorry we've got no shoes for you or underwear. But, then, you don't seem accustomed . . ."

Jake shook his head. "No matter."

"But here—I brought you a pair of me socks. They may be large." He held out a pair of black socks. Jake hesitated. "It's all right," said the young priest. "I've another pair."

Jake took them and put them on. They were several sizes too large, but why should he care? Already his toes were luxuriating in the unaccustomed warmth. They would make a layer of wool between his feet and the wet snow that seeped into his worn-out shoes. Every day that he had worked in the mill, he had helped make woolen goods for sale, but he'd never before owned anything made of wool. He nodded his thanks. He didn't know how to put it into words.

He was taken to the rectory kitchen for his supper, and what a supper it was. It was almost enough to turn a boy not only into a Catholic but to thinking seriously about becoming a priest. Did they eat like this every night? Meat and potatoes, and great slabs of bread with gravy, and three kinds of vegetables, and soup, and coffee and some kind of sweet, heavenly pudding afterward.

He didn't mind at all that he hadn't been invited to eat in the room with the big table where the priests sat but in the kitchen with Mrs. O'Sullivan. What a stroke of luck that was. She kept filling his plate and made no comment on how he ate or how much. His belly was near to bursting, but he couldn't make himself stop.

It was Father O'Reilly who brought the meal to an end. He came into the kitchen just as Jake was downing the third serving of pudding. "Still at it, are we, me boy?"

His mouth was so full, he could only nod.

"Well, that's fine. You need some meat on those bones of yours."

Jake slid his chair back from the table and stood up. He was eyeing the door, plotting a route of escape around the priest and out into the dark of the winter evening.

"No need to be afraid, lad. I don't intend to call the police."

Jake looked up, startled.

"God will hold you accountable, you know. For profaning the sacred elements and stealing from the poor." How the devil did the man know? Jake made a lunge for the door, but the priest caught him and spun him around. "I'm not through yet, me lad. You will hear me out, like it or not."

Jake didn't like it, but what choice did he have? The man's grip wasn't about to let him go. He watched half fascinated, half terrified while, with his free hand, the priest reached down into a deep pocket in his black robe. "Here," he said.

Jake's eyes nearly popped out of his head. The man was holding out a silver half dollar.

"Yes, take it. Buy some supper for the rest of your family, and then tell everyone to go back to work. This strike is the work of the devil. Tell them that. They have no business turning their children into beggars and thieves whilst they follow these godless radicals. Will you tell them that?"

Jake nodded. Though just exactly whom was he supposed to tell? His father, who hadn't worked a day in the last two years and was likely furious that Jake was not scabbing in the mill?

"And don't let me catch you in the church again unless you're praying in the pew, do you hear?"

Jake nodded furiously.

"On second thought, why don't you take your prayers to Holy Rosary? Let Father Milanese deal with you for a change. I think we've about had our fill of you here at Saint Mary's." He smiled, as though he were joking, but Jake couldn't be sure.

The priest let go his grip and gave the boy a swat on his bottom, which Jake was happy to take as a signal that he was truly dismissed with new clothes on his back and fifty cents in his fist.

Later he asked himself why a hundred times. Why, with a half dollar in his possession, did he use most of it to buy whiskey to take to his father? He must have been crazy to do such a fool thing. Yet that is exactly what he did, and almost proudly. He'd show the old man how well he was doing in the middle of this cursed strike— while others were freezing and starving, he had new clothes and money to spend on a present for his pa.

There was no one at the shack when he got there. For once he was half disappointed that his father was gone. He set the bottle right in the middle of the cot where his pa couldn't miss it and left to find a place to spend the night that wasn't a trash heap. He didn't want to ruin his new clothes quite yet.

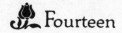 Fourteen

A Proper Caller

ROSA WASN'T GOING to school anymore. She was terrified by the idea of navigating the streets, crowded with workers and with the militia and police always present. But whenever there was soup to be had, Mamma dragged her to Chabis Hall for the meal and the meeting that followed.

Big Bill and Mrs. Gurley Flynn, along with the local strike committee members, were going around to the various halls, cheering the workers on, telling them that the union was on their side. It seemed to be true: union workers throughout the country were sending money so that the strikers could have soup for their bellies and coal for their fires. The union had a name—the Industrial Workers of the World—but no one ever called it that. If a person was feeling formal, it was the "IWW," but usually it was simply the "Wobblies." The Wobblies' motto was "Solidarity." That meant they weren't like the big unions, who represented only one kind of worker. The

Wobblies believed in standing united across various skills and national origins.

The only woman on the local strike committee was Mrs. Annie Welzenbach, who was a skilled fabric mender and a Polish Jew, to boot. The rumor was that she made more than twenty dollars a week, but that didn't stop her from siding with the lowest paid workers in the mills, Italian and Catholic though they might be. And Mrs. Welzenbach stood so tall, the police were terrified of her. "Get out on the picket line," she'd say, and thousands cheered and obeyed, turning a deaf ear to the representatives from the big-name unions who claimed that the Wobblies were lawless radicals and who warned the workers how dangerous the strike was and how futile.

Even Rosa admired Mrs. Welzenbach. Anna had told her that one time, after a march broke up, she'd seen Mrs. Welzenbach start down Common Street, probably headed home, and suddenly a couple thousand workers were marching right behind her. The militia arrested her once. They went to her house in the middle of the night and dragged her out of bed, so it was said. She was free on bail by the next afternoon and went straight to another rally. That was the day Mrs. Marino went up to her, almost throwing herself at Mrs. Welzenbach's feet, to declare: "If any hurt you, I die for you." There was something in Rosa that made her envy a woman like

Mrs. Welzenbach—young as she was and almost rich—who could inspire such loyalty.

Everyone knew she was helping lead the strike because she truly cared that people were cold and their children starving. She had told Mr. Billy Wood so right to his face, and he had turned around the next day and claimed that the strikers were being led astray by outside agitators who did not know the good relations he had always had with his workers. Mrs. Welzenbach was not an outside agitator—she was like most of them, following her parents into the mills when she was fourteen years old. But she was different from Mr. Billy Wood. She hadn't forgotten what it was like to be a poor, unskilled worker in the mills. If Rosa had been going to school, she would have told Miss Finch about Mrs. Welzenbach. Or she imagined that she would have. She might have been too timid.

She kept reading her history book over and over. If only she had the courage to go out into the street by herself, she would have gone to the library and gotten more books. She didn't want to fall too far behind in school. It was hopeless to think she could teach herself arithmetic, but she could read history and geography and books that would improve her vocabulary and strengthen her hold on English grammar, which was being buffeted daily by the various assaults on it around the kitchen table.

♣　　♣　　♣

The knock on the door came in the middle of one of Mamma's countless meetings. Rosa was lying on the bed, straining in the dim light to read the small print in the history book. At the sound, she sat up, heart pounding. The knocking stopped. None of the women in the kitchen seemed to have heard it, immersed as they were in a gabble of languages, all excited about new marches, daily meetings in the halls with the name of the brave, young Mrs. Gurley Flynn exploding into their various languages like popping corn in an iron skillet.

There was another knock, this time louder. Rosa froze. Would the police come and drag Mamma out, as they had Mrs. Welzenbach? Then a voice, muffled by the wooden door but still recognizable. "Rosa?"

Rosa, half fearful, half marveling, slid off the bed and went to open the door. There stood Miss Finch, dressed impeccably, as always, but with a flushed face and breathing hard from the exertion of climbing three flights of stairs.

"Ah, Rosa," she said, looking down into Rosa's face. "Forgive me for intruding, but you haven't been at school since . . . I don't know, too long. I was worried."

Rosa simply stared. How could she say that she'd been too frightened to go through the streets when the teacher herself had walked along those very striker-crowded and police-lined streets all the way into the

Plains, a place where people weren't feeling so friendly toward clean, well-dressed, well-fed native-born teachers?

"May I come in? Or . . . ?" The teacher was listening to the indecipherable babble from the next room.

"I'll—I'll get Mamma," Rosa said quickly, and she stepped aside to let Miss Finch into the bedroom, aware all at once of the smell of the little boys' urine-stained sheets and the sweat of an old, not too clean woman. She closed the door in a vain attempt to keep the freezing hallway from sucking out the tiny bit of heat they had. "Would you like to sit down?"

Miss Finch, without looking (it seemed to Rosa that she was making a point of not looking about her), perched herself on the edge of the big bed and smiled at Rosa.

Rosa had left the door to the kitchen partly open for what little warmth there was, so she slipped through the crack, ashamed for Miss Finch to see the group of loud shawl-clad women who were now her mother's closest friends and fellow conspirators. Mamma was leaning against the windowsill, listening to Mrs. Petrovsky's daughter interpret a lengthy harangue from her mother, whose Polish had spewed out long after her English had faltered.

Rosa slipped up beside Mamma, who almost absent-mindedly put her arm around Rosa's shoulders and drew her close, her eyes still on Mrs. Petrovsky's daughter.

"Mamma." Rosa nudged her mother's arm. "Mamma, Miss Finch is here to see you."

"Who, you say?"

"Miss Finch," Rosa whispered. "My teacher."

Mamma turned then, a puzzled expression raising her dark eyebrows. "What is teacher doing in my house?"

Rosa, still whispering, pulled on her mother's arm. "She wants to talk to you." Now several women had stopped listening to the translation of Mrs. Petrovsky's speech and had looked to see what the interruption was about.

Mamma smiled apologetically. "*Scusami,* please. A visitor only." Alarm was apparent on many faces. "No, no. No police." She took Rosa's hand, nodded at Mrs. Petrovsky's daughter, as though signaling her to carry on, and let Rosa guide her around the edge of the room into the front bedroom. Heat or no heat, Rosa closed the door behind them. The noise from the kitchen had dropped to a low murmur.

"Mrs. Serutti?" Miss Finch stood up.

"Sit, sit," Mamma said, plunking herself down on the cot opposite. "*Si,* I'm Rosa's mamma." She took Rosa's hand once more and pulled the girl down to sit beside her on the boys' bed. "Good girl, my Rosa. Smart girl, eh?"

"Yes, yes, she is, Mrs. Serutti, which is why I've come. Do you realize how long it's been since Rosa came to school?"

"A few days—a week or so, maybe?"

"The last day I have her marked present was January 29."

"That'sa day our Annie Lopizzo is shot, you know?"

Mamma had leaned forward. Rosa stiffened. Native-born weren't accustomed to having people talk right in their faces. Mamma didn't know this. She probably wasn't even aware that Miss Finch had moved slightly away; she simply leaned closer. The cot was lower than the bed, so Mamma had her head back and her chin up. Even to Rosa she looked angry. "She die, we gotta go pay respects. They don' let us go to funeral, you know."

"It was a terrible accident." Miss Finch was trying to be sympathetic. Would Mamma understand that?

"No accident." Mamma shook her head. "No accident. Militia boy shoot her down. *Pow.* Just like that. She do nothing but march, ask for bread. Then they blame us, *us*—" Mamma was pounding her chest. "They say we kill our own Annie." She made a noise with her mouth that sounded something like *pluh.* At least she didn't spit. "They say we violent"—she made the noise again. "We not killed nobody. They kill one, two—so young—" She leaned even closer toward the teacher. "That don' count all who die in mill or from sickness. We only want bread to feed our hungry children and heat to warm our freezing house and maybe some warm clothes." She stopped and studied Miss Finch's wool coat with its fur collar and her wool felt hat and the pair of leather gloves resting on her lap. "We not greedy, Teacher. We cold and starve. We gotta march or die and our children die with us."

"But is this the right way, Mrs. Serutti? Wouldn't it be better to reason with the owners?"

Mamma took her face out of the teacher's and leaned back. She closed her eyes and shook her head. "There no language they understand. Only quiet."

Miss Finch looked puzzled. "Quiet?"

"No sound. No profit. They understand that, maybe. Machine don' run itself. Wool don' weave itself. They know when the mill not making noise, is no gold clinking in the pocket. They understand that, eh?"

Miss Finch was studying Mamma as though she were a problem in arithmetic. Finally, she said, "But Rosa shouldn't march, Mrs. Serutti. It's too dangerous."

"Rosa don' march. She don' like to go out on the street. I gotta drag her to the hall to get soup so she don' starve. No, Rosa stay home. She stay home and study all day long. She got only one book, but she study one book all day long."

Rosa lowered her head. She was suddenly ashamed—too cowardly to march and too cowardly to go to school. What must the teacher think of her?

"Rosa?" The teacher's voice was kinder than Rosa had ever heard it. "How can I help you? I don't want you to fall so far behind. Olga Kronsky is still coming every day.

She lives near here. Could you walk to school together?"

That was when Mamma dropped her own dynamite. "No," she said. "Rosa no coming to school no more. She go away."

Away? What could Mamma mean?

"We send the children someplace safe." She saw Rosa's look of alarm and patted her arm reassuringly. "The union fix it. So many is sick and hungry. We can't help them here, so we send them away till we win—till we have money for food and coal and new shoes. Our children is very cold, Missa Finch. Very cold."

"Yes," the teacher murmured. "I know." She stood up and put her gloves on. "I'll look for you then, Rosa, when this is all over." She smiled. "I'll miss my best student, though." She went to the door. "Thank you, Mrs. Serutti. I'll see myself out."

They sat there on the cot, listening to the sound of Miss Finch's fine leather shoes on the stairs. They sat there until they heard the heavy front door close. Rosa waited for Mamma to explain, but Mamma just stood up, patted Rosa's head, and started for the kitchen. "I miss my meeting," she said by way of explanation and headed into the next room, leaving the door ajar to let a little heat come into the bedroom.

✿ Fifteen

The Card

"**H**EY, THERE, shoe girl."

The girl turned to see who had spoken to her in the crowded hall. There was only one person in the world who would call her "shoe girl," but Jake could tell that she didn't think he was the one. This boy had a scrubbed face and was decently dressed. His hair was a yellowish red, and his eyes were a bright blue. It tickled him to realize that there was nothing familiar about him except the name he had called her.

"Yeah, it's me, from the trash pile, remember?"

She nodded, still uncertain.

"Oh, don't worry. I didn't steal no clothes. O'Reilly caught me in his church and turned me into his good works for the day."

"*Father* O'Reilly."

"Oh, yeah, I forget, you're one of them papists, too."

The girl drew herself up as tall as possible. "*I belong to Holy Rosary parish.*"

"Sure. The Eye-talian one. That figures. . . . So, how are you?"

"Fine, thank you."

"No need to be a snip. I'm just here for soup and to warm my butt." He could tell that she was shocked by his language, but he let it pass.

"This is the Eye-talian hall, you know," she said, emphasizing the "I" just as he had.

"Didn't Joe Ettor say we was all one in this strike? What's it matter who feeds me—long as I eat?" He didn't explain that he was planning to follow Mrs. Gurley Flynn from hall to hall. Tonight she was scheduled to be at Chabis Hall. He hadn't seen her yet, just hundreds of Italians milling around, waiting for their soup. *Hell's bells*, they had a lot of kids, all of them looking half starved.

There was a stir around the doors. *She must be here.* "See ya," he said to the girl, and he pushed his way toward the entrance. No point in coming if he couldn't be up close. He wanted to be close enough to smell her. She smelled like . . . how could he tell, having lived all his life in a shack and a mill? But that day at the train station when she brushed close, he imagined that it must be the way some pretty little flower smelled. It was more intoxicating than Angelo's wine.

But Mrs. Gurley Flynn was not looking at him tonight. There was another young woman with her, and they were busy talking to the people who seemed to be in charge of the hall.

Disappointed, he faded back to where the shoe girl still stood. She was watching Mrs. Gurley Flynn, too, but not happily.

"Where's your ma?" he asked, mostly to have something to say, but also because he was curious. The two times at her flat he'd only seen her and the sister awake. The old snoring woman wasn't her ma, he felt sure. Maybe because he didn't remember his own ma, he was curious to see other people's mas. Were they kind like Mrs. Gurley Flynn, or did they box your ears and scrub your face raw? His own face still stung from the yellow soap in the rectory bath.

The girl didn't answer. He thought she hadn't heard, but then he realized she had deliberately turned away from him. *Hell's bells!* She was wiping her face, brushing away tears.

"She ain't dead?"

"No—no, she's here. Over there." She pointed to a knot of women at the edge of the crowd surrounding Mrs. Gurley Flynn and her companion. They were all jabbering away.

"Which one is she?"

"In the middle, there—in the gray shawl."

All the shawls seemed gray or so faded they could pass for gray in the dim light of the hall, but he didn't want to ask again, so he nodded, pretending to know which of the women she meant. He turned back to catch her wiping her face again. The dirt on it was streaked.

"Hey, what's the matter, shoe girl?"

"Nothing." She sniffed and straightened her shoulders.

"Then why you bawling?"

"I'm not."

"Sure you are."

"You wouldn't understand."

"How do you know? You think I'm dumb?"

"No, I think you got a lot of nerve. You're probably dying to go."

"Go? Go where?"

"My card says I'm supposed to go to New York. All the children last week went to New York."

"New York City?" His eyes danced at the thought of going to such a magical place.

"Yes. But tomorrow it may be New York or it may be some other place—Vermont somewhere."

"Vermont? Is that in the *Yew*-nited States of America?"

"Since 1791," she said primly, then her lips began to tremble. "But it's a long way from here."

"New York. Wow, wee." His head was already calculating the riches of the place. And a guy like him could get ahead there, Jake was sure of it. No more shacks by the river, no more lint-filled, stinking, steaming mill work. "Well, I ain't going to no Vermont. No, sir, I'm going to go to New York City."

"I don't think the kids get to decide. It's the parents and the committee that decide."

"What committee? I don't know nothing about no committee."

"But isn't that why you're here? To have your examination?"

"No, I come for the soup. But if anyone's going to New York City, I aim to go, too."

"You have to have a card that says so."

"What you mean, 'card'?"

"Your parents have to fill out the card and sign it, saying they want you to go and where."

Hell's bells! He should have known there'd be a catch. "How do I get me a card?"

"They won't give *you* one. They just give them to the parents."

"But s'pose . . . s'pose your ma is dead and your pa is too sick to come get a card?"

"I don't know. I wish they'd give you mine." She looked as though she might burst into tears again.

"C'mon now, c'mon. It would be *great* to go to New York City." The prospect of going to the city was suddenly the only thing in his life that rivaled the glamour of Mrs. Gurley Flynn. He was lost in a daydream of himself in the big city. He might have to start out small—selling papers, say—but it wouldn't be long before he'd be rich as Billy Wood, clever as he was. "Who gives out them cards?"

"I don't know—somebody from the union committee, I think. Mamma brought hers home from a meeting. She meant for me to go last week, but I got sick."

He looked at her and she blushed. She'd *faked* it. Why, the little trickster! But now she was caught. She was going to have to go whether she wanted to or not. "You lied, didn't you?"

"I don't know what you're talking about."

"It takes one to know one. You faked sick last week."

She tossed her head defiantly. "So?"

"So, you can help me get one of them cards now or I'm telling on you."

She bit her lip. "You're a—a—"

"Regular old bully?"

She just sighed and went over to speak to one of the gray-shawled women. The woman was holding the hand of a tiny boy, but she put her free arm around the girl's shoulders. They both turned and looked at Jake, so they were talking about him, talking about getting him one of those precious cards that would be his ticket out of Lawrence and into the greatest city in America. He knew that the streets of New York City weren't paved with gold—that was just one of those lies the foreign workers believed—but there would be chances there for a boy, and opportunity was as good as gold, now, wasn't it?

Eventually, the woman came over to where he stood, a child on each side staring at him. The little boy had eyes big as plates and a skinny little stick of a body—it was a wonder he could stand, much less walk.

"Rosa tell me your papa need a card."

"Yes, ma'am. He woulda come, but he's down real sick."

"Lotsa sick ones." The woman nodded sympathetically. "I ask for you. Go ahead, get your exam, eh? Then bring your card to the hall first thing in the morning. Okay?"

"Thank you, Mrs.—?"

"Serutti. I'm Rosa's mamma." She stroked the girl's hair. "You be good to Rosa on the train, okay? She's a little worried—go so far from home."

He promised to look after Rosa, "like a brother," he said.

After the soup, they divided the children, boys on one side of the hall, girls on the other. The woman with Mrs. Gurley Flynn examined the girls; to Jake's relief, it was a man doctor who examined the boys. The worst part was taking off his shirt and having the doctor cluck about his sunken chest and prominent ribs and then sigh deeply at the sight of his scarred back. "You do need a vacation, don't you, son?" he said.

Mrs. Serutti brought him the precious card as he was rebuttoning his shirt. "Here, boy, have your papa do it and bring it back first thing in the morning, okay? Else you can't get on the train, you understand?"

He understood. But he had no intention of taking it to his pa. He'd just scribble something on it that would look like a signature. How would anyone know it wasn't? But then he looked at the card. It was filled with words. There were lots of dotted lines that looked as though you were meant to write things down. Maybe he could scribble something that looked like somebody's name and get away with it, but all these lines? Jake couldn't read. He didn't even know what the card was asking for, much less how to write it in.

The shoe girl? Rosa? Where was she? He had to get help. He made his way to where the girls who had finished their examinations were standing and motioned her over.

She came. "Mamma got you a card, I see."

"Yeah, thanks. But could you help me? My eyes ain't too good in this light. Would you read it for me?"

She gave him a look that assured him that she knew that this time he was the faker. But she didn't say anything, she just began to read, stumbling a bit over words like "imperative" and "facilitate" that totally mystified Jake.

STRIKE COMMITTEE.
LAWRENCE TEXTILE WORKERS.

9 Mason Street.

IDENTIFICATION CARD.

It is imperative that the parents of a child, or of children, who wish to go on a vacation, during the strike of mill workers at Lawrence, Mass., give their consent in writing, and to facilitate matters they are requested to sign this identification card. No children will be accepted except the parents, father and mother, sign such a card.

Name of child ....

Age of child ....

Residence in Lawrence ....

Postal address of parents ....

Nationality ....

We, the undersigned, parents or custodians of the child above described, hereby agree that it be allowed to go on vacation to people in ....

....

in care of the "Lawrence Strikers' Children's Committee," and we agree to allow the child to stay with the friends of the strikers in that city as long as the strike will last, except that unforeseen circumstances may make the return of the child necessary before that designated time.

.... Father.

.... Mother.

.... Custodian.

Approved by the Children's Committee.

"*Cor!* How the hell could your ma even read it, much less fill it out?"

"I read the hard parts. And please, watch your language." Then her voice softened. "Can your papa read English?"

"Better'n me," he mumbled. "Couldn't your ma do it for me? Say I'm your brother or something? I mean, I'm going to be just like your brother, taking care of you on the train and all." He tried to smile in what he imagined to be a brotherly fashion.

"She won't lie for you, if that's what you mean."

"Oh, hell. I guess I gotta ask the old man, huh?"

"Look. The main thing is his signature on this line here." She pointed.

"Well, I could fake that."

"Some kids already tried. It didn't work. Just get his real signature, all right? The rest I'll help you with. We won't fake his name. It wouldn't be right."

He still had money in his pockets from the priest's handout. He stopped by the Syrian shop, which stayed open most of the night, and got more whiskey. He needed to grease the old man up before asking for anything as weighty as his signature.

The shack was pitch dark inside. "Pa?" he whispered. "You here? It's me, Jake. I brung you a treat."

No answer. He must be out. Jake felt his way to the

table. His hand found the oil lamp, but even patting the whole tabletop, he couldn't locate matches. There weren't any. He hadn't bought any for ages. He shuffled across the dirt floor to the bed. He'd just have to wait until his pa came home. He eased himself down, but when he started to push himself over to the wall, he hit something. It was Pa, lying there peaceful as the grave, not even snoring. His first thought was relief—no beating tonight. Maybe none tomorrow. And when he explained to Pa that he'd be going to New York—to *work!*—why, the old man would just jump to sign the card.

He slid under the thin quilt. *Hell's bells,* it was cold in the shack. You'd think Pa would have warmed the bed a bit by now, but then Jake had gotten soft, sleeping in churches and all. He'd clean forgot how cold the shack could be, almost as bad as a trash pile. He didn't think he could sleep, freezing as it was and excited as he was, waiting for day to come. He had to have the card signed early and get to the hall. They'd be gathering to go to the train station by nine, they'd said. So he had to be there before then. But he did fall asleep, waking with a start when light came through the dirty window and the cracks around the door.

"Pa . . . Pa," he whispered. He didn't want to wake him up too fast; it might anger him to be woken up abruptly from his sleep. Jake leaned up on his elbow and looked at his pa—stubble-bearded, his face grimy as ever—so still and peaceful. Jake had never seen him so quiet.

Something jarred inside Jake's chest. So still—too still—he was. "Pa?" Jake lay his hand on his father's arm. Then, trying hard not to panic, he cupped his hand over the man's mouth and nose. There was no hint of movement, no breath. He jumped out of the bed. "Pa!" he yelled. "Wake up! Wake up, damn you!" There was no response.

By the wall, at his father's right hand, the whiskey bottle he'd bought two days earlier lay empty. Empty as the husk on the bed. He'd slept all night with a dead body. He hadn't even had the sense to know that his pa was lying there stiff and dead beside him. *Cor,* what a fool he was.

I killed him. Didn't I wish him dead more than once? Didn't I buy the poison that done it? Jake could hardly breathe. He had to get out of there.

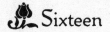 Sixteen

The Train

THE BOY HADN'T turned up at the hall the next morning. Rosa didn't know whether to be worried or relieved. He'd acted as though he really wanted to go. He must have found out she wasn't headed for New York City after all—at the last minute, Mamma had scratched out "New York City" on the card that she had filled out a week ago and had Rosa write "Barre, Vermont" in its place.

"Like a nice little village, yes? No big city for my little girl, eh? Nice people in little places, I think."

But how would the boy know that Mamma had changed her mind? He had been nowhere in sight. Even if he had seen her card, how would he know what was on it? He couldn't read—she was sure he couldn't. That thing about his eyes being too bad to see in the dim light—*Ha!* He was just ignorant. Even native-borns could be ignorant. His pa must have refused to sign. That was all she could imagine. Unless he didn't even have a father. Why would a boy who had a father be sleeping in trash piles or on someone else's kitchen floor—or getting charity from Father O'Reilly? That was it. He was an orphan. She felt sad for him, but only for a minute. Most of her pity was for herself, leaving home, leaving Mamma and Anna and Ricci. She even minded leaving the Jarusalises—a little. She wouldn't miss the smell of the little boys or the sound of Granny's snoring. But they were now part of her home, and the thought of leaving was almost more than she could bear.

If Rosa hadn't acted so cowardly, Mamma wouldn't be sending her away. Mamma wasn't sending little Ricci, and he was much thinner and punier than Rosa. Mamma should be sending Ricci. Rosa had told her so, but Mamma only said, "I can't send him away. He's just a baby, he don' understand, like you." *Like me?* Rosa wanted to say. *You think I understand why you don't want me here anymore?* But she couldn't say it out loud. Mamma wouldn't understand that as frightened as Rosa was by the strike, the thought of leaving home was much scarier. At least, during the strike she saw Mamma and Anna and knew at the end of each day that they were still safe. How was she to know that they were all right if she was far off north in an unknown place, living among strangers who didn't even know Mamma? Who might or might not tell her if anything had happened to . . . No, she couldn't think like that. She couldn't let her mind play with the possibility.

Sometimes what you imagine will happen, does, as though you made it happen.

Mrs. Gurley Flynn was asking for everyone's attention, so Rosa turned hers to the union lady who had helped think up this idea of sending her away. All the children who were leaving were surrounded by their parents and any brothers or sisters who were being left behind. As far as Rosa could see, she was one of the few children not practically dancing with excitement. The huge crowd of children going to New York were grouped together. They left first for the station. Then Mrs. Gurley Flynn gathered the Vermont-bound children and introduced them to their escorts—two men from Barre, a Mr. Broggi and a Mr. Rossi, and a man and a woman from Lawrence, neither of whom Rosa knew. The man was a Mr. Savinelli, but the woman said her name so softly that Rosa didn't hear it. Everything was taking so long, she was almost sick from waiting.

As they started for the door, Rosa heard one of the Barre men ask Mrs. Gurley Flynn where the children's coats and luggage were.

"They're wearing everything they own," she said.

"Oh," he said. "Poor children. They must be very cold." Rosa flushed with shame. She hated it, this pity from a stranger.

Mamma and Anna and little Ricci went with her all the way to the station, but none of them said much.

Little Ricci walked a few steps before begging to be carried. Mamma sighed and picked him up. "It will be good, Rosa, you see. Nice Italian people, lotsa good food, warm house. You'll like, you see." Rosa nodded numbly. Only her sister seemed to sense how very miserable Rosa was. Anna took Rosa's hand and held it tightly, squeezing it a little whenever Mamma tried to say something encouraging.

Rosa almost wished the wretched boy would show up. At least then she'd have someone to travel with. None of the children she knew seemed to be headed for Barre, Vermont. Their parents had heard all about how wonderfully the first group of children were being treated in New York City and clamored for the chance to send their own children there.

At the station, she put her face up for Mamma's kiss, then turned quickly to hide her tears.

"Alla families in Vermont is Italian, Rosa. You feel right at home, right away."

She was so tired of hearing about the good Italians of Barre, Vermont, that it was almost a relief to get on the train. Someone counted heads as they boarded the car. Rosa was number twenty-nine—twenty-nine out of thirty-five headed for the wilds of Vermont. One hundred fifty children were going to New York today. Not that she wanted to go to New York—she didn't want to go anywhere—but when they counted the New York group, she had seen Celina Cosa, not a friend exactly, but at least someone she knew from school.

By the time she got aboard, there were no more places at the windows on the station side. Mamma and Anna would be waving and waving, she knew, but she'd never see them, never get to wave back. She was shuffling toward the rear of the car, her head down, trying to stop the tears, when she spied something. It was a person, somebody curled up under the seat. No one was paying attention. Everyone else was too busy trying to find family and friends on the platform to wave to, so she leaned down. "What are you doing there?" she whispered. She knew, even from the humped back, who it was.

He could hardly turn around in the narrow space. "I got to go to New York," he said hoarsely. "I got to get out of this town."

She slid over him into the seat. She didn't have the heart to tell him that he was on the wrong train. "Why didn't you come to the hall this morning?"

"I couldn't," he croaked. "Pa didn't sign."

"Then get out from under there and get off this train. Now. Before it starts."

"I can't," he said. "You gotta help me. I can't go back there."

She took "back there" to mean Lawrence, the mill, the trash heap.

"You don't have any father," she said accusingly.

"No," he said in a choked voice, "no."

"I thought so. Well, get up and get off the train."

"I can't—really I can't. You got to believe me."

She gave a snort. When had he ever been believable?

"Besides," he said in a wheedling voice, "didn't I promise your ma I'd look after you? Like a brother, I said, remember?"

"Well, thank heavens you're not my brother."

"C'mon, shoe girl, just for today." He was pleading, begging. She didn't know what to make of it. "C'mon. I won't never bother you again. Just don't tell on me till after we get there."

The train gave a whistle and then a tremendous jerk.

"Hurry," she said. "Get off—it's starting."

"I can't," he said.

The train began a slow puffing. It was moving. There was nothing to be done. The wretched boy was headed for Vermont, like it or not.

The children who had been jammed against the windows were beginning to look around for seats. "Quick—get out from under there. Sit up here by me. They already took the count. They may not notice you."

He gave a muffled refusal.

"Well, they'll soon catch on that you don't belong if they find you trying to hide. Get up here. Now. Before everyone settles down."

He slipped out from underneath and slumped into the seat beside her. He seemed to be trying to press his body into the corner. The train was well under way now, and the noise of the engine and the wheels made her lean close so he could hear her.

"Sit up like you belong." He straightened, but only a little. "If anyone asks, you're my brother. Your name is . . ." she thought a moment. She couldn't call him Ricci, surely. "Your name is Salvatore, okay? Salvatore Serutti."

"I can't hardly say it."

"Oh, don't be such a grump. We'll call you Sal, for short. You can say Sal, can't you?"

He answered with a grunt. Something was wrong, she could sense it. He wouldn't meet her eye, and all his smart-aleck behavior had disappeared.

"What's the matter?" He shook his head. "Come on, I know something's wrong. You can tell me. Nobody will hear over the train." He shook his head again, still not looking at her. They rode on in silence for a while, listening to the *clack, clack, clack* of the wheels against the rails. She'd never ridden a train before, and oddly enough, she liked it. They chugged past buildings and houses and then, gathering speed, seemed to whiz by the fields beyond the town. The snow out there in the open country was so different from the gray slush in the city, like a pure white wool blanket tucked cozily about the farms.

"Isn't it beautiful?"

He seemed to shake himself out of a stupor. "What you say?"

"The snow out here, the fields, the little houses and barns . . ."

He glanced out the window and then away. "I s'pose."

"Come on, Sal, what's the matter?"

"My name ain't Sal. That's a girl's name."

She smiled inwardly. She didn't dare let him know how relieved she was to see a bit of his old spirit. "Not in Italian. It's a very good boy's name. Besides, I don't even know your real name. You never told me."

"Don't matter now. I reckon I'm Sal—least till I get to New York."

She felt a pang for the disappointment she was about to deliver. "Sal . . . we aren't—we aren't going to New York."

He sat straight up and looked right into her face. "Where the hell *are* we going?"

"To—to Vermont."

"Hell's bells!" He sagged so low, his spine went almost off the edge of the seat. "Why didn't you tell me?"

"I told you to get off the train. Remember? And you wouldn't."

"I thought it was because I didn't have no stinking card."

That had been the reason, but, all the same . . . "You

didn't ask me where the train was going. You were already here when I got on, remember?"

"I seed you, and I seed you was going to get on this train. I know there was two groups, but you said you was going to New York."

Of course, he hadn't been able to read the signs. "That was yesterday. Mamma changed the card last night. She thought a small place would be better for me. Not so scary."

"I don't have no luck, do I? Nothing but stinking bad luck all my stinking life."

"Maybe you'll like it in Vermont."

He gave her a withering look. "I'd sooner go to hell."

"You don't mean that!"

"You don't know me so good. *Cor!* What am I gonna do?" He was muttering to himself now, the gloom once again enveloping him like a thick fog.

The woman escort was coming down the aisle with slabs of bread and cheese that she was handing out to each child.

Oh, mercy, was she counting? Rosa began to prepare her speech about the brother who had been added at the last minute. But there was no need. The woman just smiled and gave her two slices of bread with cheese.

"For when he wakes up," she said, indicating the boy, who was now leaning against the corner with his eyes closed.

Rosa nodded, trying to smile back. "Thank you," she said in a small voice.

The woman turned to the other side to distribute lunch to the children across the aisle. Rosa waited until the escort had finished and returned to her seat at the front of the car. Then she punched Sal—well, he would have to be Sal from now on. "Sal, here's some lunch for you."

"I ain't hungry," he said, crossing his arms and hugging his chest, his eyes still shut.

"Of course you are. It's bread and cheese. The bread is fresh, too." She took a bite and began to chew elaborately. "*Mmm*, very good."

He opened an eye and stuck out his hand. She gave him his share of the bread and cheese and watched him take a small bite. Soon he was wolfing it down. He *was* hungry. Weren't they all?

"Isn't that better? Don't you feel better now you've had something to eat?"

"Don't ask me how I feel, all right?" he said, wiping his mouth with the back of his hand. "Just leave me alone."

She leaned back against the seat. It had a white piece of cloth just above where she rested her head. It was clean, like the country snow. There was something comforting about someone washing those cloths where people put their heads. Maybe the strange place she was going to would be clean, too. She knew Mamma tried, but how could you ever win against the smoke from the city's chimneys? It was always dirty at home, and clean water was hard to come by.

She didn't try to talk to the boy again. She thought about home, about Mamma—Mamma singing in the street, her voice so pure and strong. Everyone wanted Mamma to lead the singing. She could have been an opera singer if she'd stayed in Italy, Rosa imagined. She said that once to Mamma, who had only laughed. "You need money to be singer, Rosa. You need lesson, you need piano for practice. We don't have no thing like that."

It wasn't fair for some people to have so much, and others not even enough to eat. That was why Mamma was striking. Rosa knew that. But there was no way they could win. They were too weak and the owners too strong. They would starve or freeze long before the owners gave in. And the card that Mamma had signed said: "as long as the strike will last." *As long as the strike will last.* Mamma and Anna and little Ricci were likely to be dead before it was all over. She could feel the tears gathering, and she squinched her eyes to hold them back. She didn't want that wretched boy to catch her crying, not when she was pretending to be the strong one.

Someone near the front of the car began to sing and was soon joined by many of the children on board:

"We shall not be, we shall not be moved.
We shall not be, we shall not be moved.
Like a tree planted by the water . . ."

She couldn't help it. All she could hear was Mamma's beautiful voice soaring over everyone else's. The tears she had dammed up behind her eyelids burst through. She buried her face in her hands and tried to stifle the sobs that were shaking her body.

"Hey, hey, shoe girl. Cut it out. Vermont ain't going to be *that* bad. You said so yourself."

She shook her head. "I'm not crying about Vermont."

"Well, what, then?"

"Nothing." Suddenly, she felt a bit of the lost bravado returning. "None of your business, and my name is *Rosa*."

"Okay. Have it your way." He slumped back into his corner, once again crossing his arms tightly across his chest and closing his eyes.

The singing went on, from one union song to the next. All the children seemed to know the words. Rosa knew them, too, but her throat was far too tight to join in even if she'd felt like singing.

The big man from Barre called Mr. Broggi stood up to announce that the train was running late. Rosa sighed. The ride had seemed endless once the novelty had worn off. Even the snow-covered mountains, which made Rosa

sit up and stare out the window, had lost their enchant-
ment after a while. She wanted to get off the train. If she
couldn't go home, she wanted to know what was next—
and the long train ride was like traveling through limbo.
You weren't anywhere when you were on a train, she
decided. You weren't where you had been, and you
weren't yet where you were going. You were nowhere. It
might be beautiful outside the window—and it was, she
had sense enough to realize that—but it wasn't anywhere
to her, just a scene passing by that was framed by the
train window.

Mr. Broggi stood up again. "We be there soon," he
said. "Thank you for your patience. The workers and their
families who will be your hosts will all be at the station to
meet you. I tell you for sure they're eager as you for this
train to arrive. They've made a feast at the hall, so we
don't bring more food for the.train. There'll be plenty of
supper after we get there, I promise, and very warm welcome to Vermont."

The boy muttered something under his breath,
which Rosa couldn't hear and probably wouldn't have
wanted to.

At last, the train gave an ear-piercing whistle and
began to slow down. The children on the station side
pressed their faces to the windows for their first glimpse
of Barre, Vermont. Instead of endless stretches of giant
factories, all Rosa could see from her window were

strange horseshoe-shaped buildings with train tracks running right into them. It was almost dusk, but there was enough daylight to see how different this little town was from Lawrence. The snow was still white here and deeper on the rooftops.

"Look! Look!" the children on the station side were calling out. "Look at all the people. It's like a march."

Rosa's heart gave a thump. Not strikes here, too. Surely not. She'd been sent away to get free from strikes.

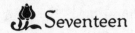 Seventeen

At the Labor Hall

JAKE PLANNED HIS next moves while still aboard the train. As soon as he got off, he'd disappear into the crowd. Somewhere, somehow, he'd be able to get enough money to buy a ticket to New York City, or Boston at least. He couldn't stay in this dump town, that was certain. Even if they didn't catch on, even if they thought he belonged, he couldn't stay. Someone was sure to find Pa's body. Someone was sure to know about him. Even if the police didn't pick him up for murder—his heart almost stopped beating at the thought—*even if* the police didn't accuse him, they'd know, wouldn't they, that he was at fault. They'd send him to some orphanage—which, he knew, would be worse than prison.

With luck, the weather would stay cold a good while longer. But when spring came, as it always did, a passer-by would be sure to smell the corpse. Jake had smelled plenty of rotting animals; he knew the stench. Or maybe some stray dogs would break into the shack. . . . He nearly vomited at the thought. Oh, God, what was he to do? But first things first. Shake the girl, slip through the mob at the station, and find someplace in this one-horse town to hide until he could make a plan for escape.

They were almost the last of the children off the train, but as soon as he stood on the steps, before he put his first foot on the station platform, he knew he wouldn't try to run that night. The freezing air that hit his face was like none he'd ever felt. Where in the hell was Vermont? At the North Pole? Besides, the girl was holding on to his arm for dear life.

The crowd was not nearly the size of the crowd that had greeted Big Bill and beautiful Mrs. Gurley Flynn, but it looked as though it must be most of the town. There were signs, just as though the people were marchers, but the signs were held up and waved by smiling, warmly dressed people, many of whom sported bright red ribbons. Of course, he couldn't read the signs.

"That one says, BENVENUTI." The shoe girl was reading his mind. "Just like the one over there in English, see?" She had let go of his arm and was pointing out the signs in Italian, pretending it was only those that he couldn't read. "They all say, WELCOME or WELCOME, LAWRENCE CHILDREN. Just like the ones in English."

The crowd was being urged back so the children could pass through it directly and into the autos, trucks, and livery wagons that were backed up to the platform.

The girl stiffened and hesitated at the side of the auto they were being ushered toward, but Jake grabbed her arm and pulled her onto the running board and into the back seat. The engine was loud and the fumes smelly, but at least they'd be going in style—wherever they might be headed. It would only be for one night, he promised himself. As soon as he could beg or steal money for a train ticket, he'd be gone . . . if they didn't catch him first.

The driver turned toward the back seat and smiled warmly. *"Buona sera!"* he said.

Cor! Was Italian going to be the language in this town? How in the world would he manage? Even to skip town you had to be able to speak to somebody.

"We welcome you to Barre. We are expecting you so many days."

Whew! The man could speak English, which gave Jake some hope for the rest of the town.

"By the door, there, is a blanket if you're cold."

"Grazie," the girl murmured.

Oh, hell. Was she going to go into Italian or was she just showing off? No, she was shivering too hard for that. He took the blanket from the corner of the seat and tucked it around them right up to their chins. The driver smiled and nodded.

"First we have a little welcome parade," he said. "Then we go to Labor Hall for a *beeeg* feast. You like that?"

"Si," the girl said.

He wished she'd shut up with the Italian. What was she trying to prove? He was thinking up what to say when the doors opposite them opened, and two other children were crowded in beside them on the back seat while another climbed in beside the driver up front.

"*Andiamo!* Let's go," the driver said, and did something that made the motor cough and the auto jerk forward. The girl gave a little muffled cry.

"It's a motorcar!" The child sitting on the other side of Rosa was exultant.

"Yeah?" Jake muttered. "You ain't never seen one?"

"I never *rided* in one!" the little boy said.

Neither had Jake, but, *cor,* the kid's wide-eyed wonder was worse than the shoe girl's terror. It made them all sound like they were just out of steerage. Like they were more backward than the dumb wops in this one-horse town. *Oh, Christmas.* It hit him. For the rest of the time that he was stuck here, *he* would be one of those wops just off the boat. *Sal—Sal . . . hell's bells,* he couldn't even say his own stupid name.

The little kid who'd yelled about the motorcar now stood up, pushed his way past Rosa, and was leaning across Jake's knees to stick his head out the opening above the door. "It's a real parade," he said. "We're in a real parade!"

"That's right, son. Everybody in town come to see you and say, 'Hello! Welcome to Barre in Vermont.'"

"To see *us*?" His voice was so shrill, it pierced Jake's skull like a mill whistle.

"Just you, nobody else."

They were bumping along on what must be the main street, if a town this size had such a thing. Anyhow, there were stores on either side and people lined up in front of them, waving Italian and American flags and yelling and clapping as they went by. There were bands playing as well. Jake didn't know the tunes, but the music was not too bad, and as it got louder, nobody tried to talk, which was a relief.

They followed the livery in front of them around a tiny common, which was nearly surrounded by churches. There were people standing in the snow even on the common, waving signs and yelling. Then their little parade headed back down the street the same way it had come.

"Ouch! Would you get off my foot?" The kid was not only standing on Jake's foot, he was jumping up and down on it in his excitement, but the boy either didn't hear Jake or just chose to ignore him. Jake picked him up and plopped him down on the seat next to Rosa. "He was killing me," he explained, but Rosa didn't indicate that she had heard. She was staring straight ahead, her eyes wide with fright. "I didn't hurt him. See? He's all right." The little boy had jumped right up and now was crowding the little girl who was standing at the opening on the other side.

They passed the street leading back to the station and turned into a narrower one a little way farther on. By the time the driver stopped the auto, it was truly night. Night came early up here, it seemed.

"Okay," the driver said. "Here we are. The feast is waiting."

The three smaller passengers leaped out of the auto and joined the crowd of children hurrying up the stone steps that led to the brick building, which must be the Labor Hall the driver had mentioned earlier. Rosa was still sitting there on the seat, as though frozen in place. Jake punched her elbow. "We're here now. Get out."

She stumbled toward the open door, onto the running board, and then down to the street. He followed her, and the two of them walked up the steps into the hall.

The smell of food was what hit Jake first. The glorious smell of meat and garlic and hot, fresh-baked bread. He'd thought, on the train, that he'd never have any appetite again, just thinking of Pa's dead body and what might become of it—as well as what might become of him when it was found. But he was hungry, hungry enough to eat an automobile if it was covered with enough meatballs and tomato sauce.

There were people at the door greeting everyone, both in Italian and in English. Jake almost burst out for one of the long tables, but he was stopped and sent to one end of the hall. Rosa was sent to the other end. *Hell's bells,* hadn't a doctor just cluck-clucked over him a few hours ago? But there was nothing to do but to wait his turn while a local doctor listened through his little rubber thing and thumped his back and looked down his throat and into his ears.

A young man was standing by the doctor, checking names off the list. What was Jake to do? His name wasn't going to be on any list.

"What's your name, son?" the young man asked.

"Oh," Jake said, "I ain't on no list. My sister—see, that girl over there with the— Wait, I'll get her. She can explain."

The man looked puzzled, but he didn't try to stop Jake from running across the hall and grabbing Rosa by the arm. "You gotta come," he said. "I ain't on the list."

He was glad to see that she seemed to have recovered from the terror of the auto ride. "Oh, honestly," she said, but she came with him to speak to the man holding the fateful list.

"I—I wouldn't leave unless my brother came with me this morning, so he snuck on board. Mamma will know where he is. She wanted him to come to look after me."

The man raised his eyebrows. "And your name, young fellow?"

"Uh—Sal—"

"Salvatore. He hates it. He wants everyone just to call him 'Sal.'"

"All right, Sal, but we need to have your whole name."

"Serutti." Rosa jumped in quickly. "Same as me."

"Salvatore Serutti," he said and then smiled. "Just for the list, all right? Otherwise, we call you Sal." He wrote something down on the board. "Have you had your examination, Miss Serutti?"

"Rosa," she said, smiling prettily, like a picture. "Yes. I have." What a faker!

"Then you're all set. Go find yourselves seats at the tables. The food is coming as soon as we finish the examinations and check everyone in."

"Well, you could at least thank me," she muttered as they headed for the nearest open seats.

"Okay," he said. "Thank you. Now are you satisfied?"

She just sighed. "Just behave yourself, all right? I can't help you if you don't try to behave."

But Jake was paying no attention. His eyes were following the line of women emerging from a room at the end of the hall. Each was carrying either a pot or a huge platter, which she then set down on one of the tables. There were round tubelike noodles big as his finger covered with tomato sauce. There was a platter with hunks of sausage swimming in tomato sauce. There were huge plates of juicy pieces of chicken so tender they were falling off the bone. There wasn't the spaghetti that he thought Italians ate with every meal, but a dish of something that wasn't potato but not pasta, either.

"What's this stuff?" he asked Rosa.

"Polenta," Rosa whispered. "Taste it. It's good."

Good? Jake bet the angels in heaven didn't have anything that tasted half this good.

There were baskets of bread—thick, crusty slices of it—and smaller platters with cheese and salami and olives and all sorts of strange things. Jake didn't pay much attention to these—he was loading his plate with chicken and polenta and meat sauce, none of that other foreign stuff he didn't recognize. A meal like this ought to last him a few days. Now all he needed was enough money to get himself out of here.

The bands had followed them right into the hall, and while they ate, the musicians played cheerful tunes. Every now and then, between the food and the music, Jake would forget all about the troubles he was running from.

The feast ended with cakes and sweets. Jake stuffed some of the candies into his pocket when Rosa wasn't looking. He knew she'd object if she saw him do it.

"Now, boys and girls," the big man who had been on the train was saying in a booming voice. "Let me ask you. Have you had enough to eat?" A few scattered yeses and thank-yous were heard. The man cupped his hand against one ear. "I can't hear you. . . . Have you had enough to eat?"

"YES!" the children thundered back.

"Good," he said. "We don't want no child hungry tonight. Now you will meet your hosts for your visit in Barre. Is everyone excited?"

"YES!"

"Good. I can promise you all the people in Barre are excited, too. I bring here only thirty-five children, and many, many more families want to be hosts." He shook his head. "So now, Mr. Marchesi, please to call out names from the list, and the family that has this name, come meet your guest, all right?"

"Gladly, Mr. Broggi." The same young man who had checked names off the list earlier stepped up and began reading the names of the children. Not all the names were Italian, Jake realized. He could have kept his own name, except that he couldn't be Rosa's brother with a name like Jake Beale. His heart thumped as each name was called. What was the man going to do when he got to Rosa's name? But he needn't have worried. "Rosa and Salvatore Serutti," the man called out, just as though his peculiar name had always belonged on the list.

"Stand up!" Rosa commanded. He got to his feet, looking around for the people that would come forward to claim them. At first, no one seemed to move.

"Rosa and Salvatore Serutti?" Mr. Marchesi repeated, looking around as well.

A woman was moving toward them. She looked ancient to Jake, all white hair and wrinkles, a shawl wrapped around her body. Several steps behind her was a tiny man. He was no taller than a child, but not a child at all, for he had a head of snow-white hair and a great white mustache sprouting from his upper lip like a snow-covered bush.

They came slowly from the far corner of the hall to where Mr. Marchesi stood holding the list. The woman turned and waited for the old man to catch up with her, and when he did, he muttered something in Italian to Mr. Marchesi.

"What did he say?"

"He said he didn't ask for any boy," Rosa whispered back.

Eighteen

The Gerbatis

JAKE ALMOST PANICKED. If the old man didn't take him, what would happen? He'd be separated from Rosa and stuck with some family that probably didn't even speak English.

"Mr. Gerbati," Mr. Marchesi began, but Rosa interrupted whatever he was about to say.

"*Scusami, Signor—*" She was putting on her saddest, prettiest little face. He'd probably never know whatever it was she said to the old man, but he could see the old lady's face soften.

"Oh," she murmured, "*povera bambina,*" and she put her arm around Rosa's shoulders.

"There are many families who would be glad—" said Mr. Broggi, but the woman interrupted him.

"We fine, Signor Broggi. Is okay."

The old man was defeated. Jake could see that. Without speaking another word, he started for the door. There was a coat rack beside it from which he took an overcoat and a fedora. Then he led them outside and down the stone steps. Mrs. Gerbati followed, her arm still around Rosa's shoulders, with Jake trailing behind. Mrs. Gerbati stopped on the top step, took the shawl off her own shoulders, and wrapped it around Rosa. She turned and smiled at Jake, as if to apologize for not having another to give him. The old man never glanced around. He was down the steps already and, shoulders straight as a sergeant major, was marching up the middle of the street where most of the snow had been cleared away from the cobblestones.

It was obvious that Mr. Gerbati didn't own an automobile or even have access to a livery. Why couldn't they have gone home with their parade driver? Not this glum old man. The walk to the Gerbati house took only a few minutes, but Jake truly thought he might be frozen to the stone street before they got there. His shoes had never been much protection, but they were of no use at all here, and the wind went straight through the shirt and trousers the priest had given him.

Mr. Gerbati reached the house before the others, and he stood, waiting on the porch, stiff as a telegraph pole. The house was hard to make out in the dark, but it loomed large. They went inside, and Mr. Gerbati closed the door, took off his fedora, and hung it on a huge piece of furniture in the front hall. They followed him into a room off the hall to the right, where there were chairs, a couch, and a squat iron stove.

Mrs. Gerbati murmured something to her husband. He nodded curtly, thrust a heaping shovelful of coal into the stove, and stirred the fire, making the flame blaze up. The children looked at each other, their eyes wide in amazement. An entire shovelful of coal! And nearly bedtime, at that.

"Come, come close." Mrs. Gerbati motioned Jake toward the stove. She turned and said something in Italian to Rosa, which must have meant, *Doesn't your brother speak Italian?* because Rosa was smiling apologetically. "He wants to be only American," she said in English. "So he's forgotten all his Italian."

"Forgot?" Mrs. Gerbati shook her head sadly. "Must not forget, Salvatore, must not." It didn't seem the time to tell Mrs. Gerbati that he wanted to be called "Sal."

The old man hadn't said a word yet. He sat down in a large chair, lit a pipe, and watched as though he were at a performance of some sort as his wife bustled about. Rosa and Jake stood awkwardly, not speaking, not daring to look at the old man as their hostess disappeared into the kitchen. A few minutes later she reappeared with a tray of steaming cups. "Just a little *vino,* warm against the cold, *si?*"

"*Grazie,*" Rosa said.

"*Grazie,*" Jake echoed, making the old woman beam

with pleasure. He took the cup and held it, trying to steal some of its heat for his frozen fingers.

When Mrs. Gerbati took Rosa upstairs to go to bed, Jake had another moment of panic. They hadn't been expecting a boy, just a girl. Where would they put him? But he needn't have worried. There was a tiny room with a narrow bed off the kitchen. Mrs. Gerbati gave him a flannel shirt that must belong to her husband and told him to put it on. She left while he changed, and then came in and made up the bed with gleaming white sheets, quilts, even a pillow. He started to get under the covers. "*No, no, aspetta.* Wait!" She hurried into the kitchen and brought back some kind of long-handled contraption, which she rubbed up and down between the sheets. "Now," she said. "Is nice for you."

He sank into the comfort of the warm bed. Auto or no auto, the Gerbatis must be rich. This big house, a mattress beneath him, and soft, fat quilts on top of him. Soon, even his frozen feet began to tingle, and before he could worry about what might happen the next day or the next, he was fast asleep.

"Sal . . . Sal, wake up."

His eyelids felt glued together. It took him a moment to remember where he was—floating, as he seemed to be, upon a heated cloud. He grunted and turned his back on the intrusion, but Rosa, curse her, persisted.

"It's Sunday."

"Go away."

"Mrs. Gerbati wants to take us to Mass. She says she owes it to Mamma to see we go."

"I ain't Catholic."

"You are as far as they know."

"Tell her I'm tired and I got to rest today."

"Yes, maybe that's better. I don't want you to pretend to be Catholic. You got too much sin on your soul to add that."

He sat up now. How would *she* know about Pa? "What do you mean?"

"Oh, Sal, you know perfectly well. You lie, you cheat, you steal. I don't know how many mortal sins—"

She was just guessing. She didn't know anything about that body in the shack. He shivered and slid back under the covers.

"You really don't look well. If you need anything, Mr. Gerbati has just gone to fetch his newspaper. He'll be right back."

Hell's bells. He was hoping to have the house to himself. The rich old buzzard probably had a load of cash stashed under some mattress. That's what everyone said foreign-borns did, believing as they did that banks would steal their money. "I won't bother him none."

"We'll have breakfast when we get back—if you're up to eating."

He'd be up to eating, all right, just not up to trying to talk to the old man.

Rosa hadn't gone to confession, so she sat in the pew when Mrs. Gerbati went forward to receive the host. She should have been saying her Our Fathers, but instead she was trying to figure out what she could do about the boy . . . Sal. The name didn't fit him in the least. He looked no more like a Salvatore than a pigeon. He didn't look Italian at all. He looked like an orphaned mill boy, probably not Irish, since he had no respect for Father O'Reilly, but native-born, with no religion at all, judging by his language. And why had he suddenly turned all funny? Yesterday on the train he'd acted as though he thought somebody was after him. The police? Had he done something so bad that the law was after him? If so, he wasn't the only one in trouble. Hadn't she helped him get away? That was as bad as doing the crime yourself, wasn't it? To help a criminal escape arrest? Her heart was thumping madly now. And Mamma had sent her up here so she would be safe. *Oh, Mamma, if you only knew.*

How was she going to make him behave? He'd said he'd disappear as soon as they got off the train. He'd practically promised that she wouldn't have to put up with him any longer than the ride itself. And yet here they were, brother and sister in the Gerbatis' house. Mrs. Gerbati was so kind, but Mr. Gerbati . . . It was obvious that he wanted little to do with her and even less to do with the boy.

Maybe she should have disowned him last night, refused to help when the man was checking the list. That's what, she now realized, she should have done. Then it would be someone else's problem—what to do with him. She wouldn't be caught in a web of lies and pretense and who knew what else.

What should she do? She was so mixed up. And here came sweet old Mrs. Gerbati down the aisle, smiling at her so kindly, so lovingly, so trustingly.

On the walk back to the house, Mrs. Gerbati explained apologetically that her husband didn't attend Mass. "*Socialisto,*" she said. "In Carrara the priest say he cannot be Catholic and socialist, too. So he choose. No more church. But good man, you see. Even is artist."

Rosa had thought all the men in Barre were granite workers. How could you be an artist, digging stone out of the ground? Maybe she'd misunderstood. She felt shy about asking. She didn't want Mrs. Gerbati to think she was doubting the woman's word about her husband.

After breakfast, which Sal, miraculously cured, was able to put away at an almost alarming rate, Mr. Gerbati went to the sitting room to read his morning paper. Once her husband was settled in his chair, Mrs. Gerbati took Jake by the arm. "Come, come," she said. "You, too, Rosa."

Through the open door, Mr. Gerbati looked up briefly from his paper but didn't speak, though Rosa thought for a minute he might.

"*Scusami, per favore,*" Rosa murmured. She followed Mrs. Gerbati out of the kitchen into the hall and up the wide flight of stairs and another narrower flight into what must be the attic. She'd read about attics in books, but she'd never actually been in one. It was amazing to see the size of this house in which only two elderly people lived.

The space was under the eaves of the house, lit poorly by a small window at one end. It was empty, except for a couple of trunks and a few wooden crates. Mrs. Gerbati went to one of the trunks and opened it. A strong woody smell filled the musty air. Kneeling beside the trunk, the woman felt about in the depths. She pulled out several garments, studying each, glancing at Sal, and then putting some back, some into a pile on the open trunk lid. Finally, she gathered up the pile in one arm and turned, still kneeling, toward the children. Rosa stared. There were tears on the old woman's face. Mrs. Gerbati wiped her face hastily with the tail of her apron. Then she gave a laugh and reached out her free hand toward Sal. "*Aiutami, per favore,*" she said.

"She needs your help to get up," Rosa whispered to the boy. "Give her your hand."

Sal pulled the old lady to her feet.

"Now," Mrs. Gerbati said, heading for the attic steps. "We see."

What Mrs. Gerbati wanted to see, it seemed, was whether the clothes she had taken out of the trunk would fit Sal. She bypassed the sitting room and led them directly into the kitchen. Then she sent Jake to his room with the armload and ordered him to try everything on. After he'd disappeared into his room, she went to the sink and began to fill a basin with a mixture of water from a kettle on the stove and water from the tap above the sink. Rosa hurried to the table to carry over the breakfast dishes—twice as many dishes for the four of them as the nine members of the Serutti-Jarusalis household would ever own, let alone use in one meal. It hurt her to think of her hungry family. If only she could send them a bit of the Gerbatis' food and a few shovelfuls of coal.

Soon Sal appeared at the door separating his room from the kitchen. He had on a wool cap and an oversized heavy wool overcoat. His face was hardly visible behind the coat's thick collar.

"Now, take off, let's see," Mrs. Gerbati ordered.

Sal took off the cap and unbuttoned the overcoat and put them down on a kitchen chair.

Rosa gasped. The boy was dressed finer than a mill owner's son in a wool suit with a white shirt underneath. The pants and sleeves of the suit were too long for him, but Mrs. Gerbati had already hurried over to kneel beside him and start to turn up the cuffs on the trousers. "I fix, I fix," she said. "Then perfect, yes?"

"*Che stai facendo?*" The cry from the opposite doorway made the children jump in fright. They hadn't even seen the little man until he shouted, a shout that sounded to Rosa less like an angry person than an animal in pain.

His wife turned and began to make soothing noises in Italian that even Rosa couldn't understand. Sal just stood there in his magnificent clothes, his eyes wide. Mrs. Gerbati stuck out her hand, so Rosa ran over to pull her to her feet. The old woman nodded her thanks and then went to the door and gently pushed her husband back into the front room, shutting the door behind her. Rosa and Sal were left staring at each other, unable to figure out what was being said on the other side of the wall except to know that it was one between a wounded man and a woman trying desperately to soothe him.

"What have we done?" Rosa said. "What have we done?"

"We ain't done nothing," Sal said. "It was her done it. I didn't ask for nothing. It was her fault."

"She did it *for* us, don't you see?"

After what seemed like an eternity, the door opened and Mrs. Gerbati returned. "Better to take off," she indicated the clothes. "Not so good. We buy new clothes for you tomorrow, yes?" Without another word, she returned to the sink and finished washing the last of the dishes, handing each dish to Rosa, who polished and repolished every piece.

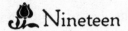 Nineteen

New Clothes and New Problems

IT HAD BEEN a glum morning. After his outburst, Mr. Gerbati returned to his chair in the sitting room and buried himself in his paper. But even worse in Rosa's mind was the change in Mrs. Gerbati. All the warmth had slipped away. She put away the clean dishes without talking or smiling—just a nod and a murmured *grazie* for Rosa's help. Then she went to sit in the front room herself, taking up some kind of sewing job. Through the open door, Rosa could see her glance up from time to time, sending a worried look in her husband's direction.

Sal reappeared, looking thin and drab in his own clothes, and plunked himself down at the kitchen table. Rosa sat across from him, fiddling with the fringe of the tablecloth that hung onto her lap. What had happened? She wanted to talk to Sal, but with the door to the sitting room wide open, she was afraid to speak aloud. She cleared her throat. He ignored her, seeming to study his chapped hands and grimy, broken fingernails.

"I think I'll go up to my room," she said finally. There was no answer, so she pushed back her chair and stood up. He didn't raise his head. "So," she said. "I guess I'll just go."

"Fine," he said. "Go."

"Okay. I'm going."

"Hell's bells," he said in a voice too low to be heard in the next room. "Just get out of here, will you?"

Rosa bit her lip. She slipped from the kitchen into the hall to avoid passing through the sitting room, where the Gerbatis sat in grim silence.

She climbed the stairs and went into the room Mrs. Gerbati had fixed for her and shut the door. There was a lot of furniture for one person: a wide bed, a bureau with drawers, a washstand with a large white basin and tall pitcher, and a little rocker decorated with an embroidered cushion. There was a lace-curtained window that looked out onto the quiet street with its snow-covered yards and bushes and bare branches. It was a room all to herself, with no bedwetting little boys, and a bed that did not have to be shared with anyone. It should have been wonderful, but she had never felt so lonely in her life. *Oh, Mamma, why did you send me away?* She lay face down on the quilt and cried until the pillow was soaked.

"Rosa?" Mrs. Gerbati was tapping on the door.

Rosa sat up. "Yes?"

"Please to come in?"

Rosa wiped her face on the back of her hand. "Yes, yes, of course."

Mrs. Gerbati entered the room by degrees. First just her head, then her shoulders, and then finally she pushed the door open enough to get her whole body into the room.

"You cry, *povera bambina*. Please, no cry, no cry." She came over to the bed and stroked Rosa's hair and then her cheek, as though to wipe away her tears, ignoring the ones streaking her own face.

Rosa snuffled. "I'll be all right. I just miss my mamma."

"*Si, si.* Is very hard to leave your mamma far away. Mr. Gerbati and me, we be Papa and Mamma now, okay?"

What could Rosa say? That the last thing Mr. Gerbati seemed to want was to be their papa?

"This morning—" Mrs. Gerbati said. "You know, this morning I make big mistake. I wrong. Not you. Not Salvatore." She sighed deeply. "Only me."

"The clothes?"

The woman nodded. "Our boy. He die many years ago. Mr. Gerbati still"—she patted her heart—"still sick, in here."

Rosa knew. She was still sick "in here" from Papa's death.

"I like to have boy in my house again, but he say no

good. I make big mistake, put Vittorio's clothes on Salvatore, you know?" She slammed a fist into her chest. "Like arrow straight to heart. You tell Salvatore, yes?" She waved her hand. "Not Salvatore fault. You tell him, okay?"

Rosa nodded. "I'll explain."

"Tomorrow, first thing, we buy new clothes. Now, we eat. Time for *colazione*."

Rosa nodded, although it seemed they'd only just finished breakfast.

"Then we go to Labor Hall to get"—she squinted her eyes and made a squeezing gesture with her right hand— "*una fotografia* for Mamma!" She smiled broadly. "She be so happy to see Rosa and Salvatore in *foto*, yes?"

They were going to take pictures to send to Mamma? Rosa should have been pleased, but what would Mamma think when she saw Sal's face in the photograph?

Mr. Gerbati didn't go with Rosa and Jake to the Labor Hall, but Mrs. Gerbati did, clucking all the way like a mother hen. Jake, even with Rosa's explanation of the old man's behavior, couldn't shake a feeling of dread. He didn't care about the stupid photograph—he'd be gone long before Rosa's mother ever saw it—but he couldn't get over Mr. Gerbati's scream. It was too much like— well, like he'd been found out, that somehow the old man knew his secret and wanted him gone even before

Jake could figure out how to make his getaway. He would have to wait at least until the old lady bought him some clothes. It was a waste, really. All those swell clothes in the attic, and yet . . . and yet they had belonged to a dead boy. He shivered. It was just as well. He already had too much of the smell of death on him.

Some of the kids milling around in the hall were wearing jackets and hats they hadn't been wearing the day before. He could have looked as good as they did if Mr. Gerbati hadn't raised that fit this morning. Jake pretended not to notice the neat suits on the other boys. He and Rosa weren't going to be wearing hand-me-downs. They were going to have brand-new clothes from a fancy store. So there. Who cared about these stupid pictures anyway?

He and Rosa were told to stay in one spot to wait their turn to be taken out on the steps of the hall for their photograph. Mr. Broggi warned everyone not to move. "You move," he said, "your photo look like big smear." Several photographers stood at street level behind their big long-legged cameras, holding the rubber bulbs in their right hands, from time to time ducking under the black cloths draped over the cameras, then jumping out to squeeze their bulbs and cry in English or Italian, "Hold still!" *"Bene!"* "Good!" *"Un' altre volta!"* "Once more now!" "Next!"

As soon as the photographer yelled, "Hold still!" Jake

quickly turned his head. If his face was just a smear, nobody would be able to make out who he was.

"Next!" Jake took Rosa's arm and pulled her quickly back up the steps and into the building. Mr. Marchesi, who was once again the list holder, was waiting at the door. Rosa gave him her mamma's name and address, and then they went over to the edge of the room.

"I don't know what Mamma's going to say when she sees your picture."

"She won't know who it is. I moved. I'll be a smear. She'll just think it's a bad photo."

Rosa didn't look convinced.

"Have you all had a picture taken for your parents?" Mr. Marchesi asked. The children murmured assent. "Then we want all thirty-five of you out on the steps for a group picture with your official escorts from Barre and Lawrence."

Jake and Rosa looked at each other. What would happen if someone in Lawrence or Barre were to count heads in the photograph and find an extra child? Seeing the panic in Rosa's eyes, Jake melted into the back of the crowd, and as everyone else headed for the front steps, he slipped into the kitchen. He leaned hard against the door until he heard the noisy crowd of children coming back into the hall. Then opening the door a crack, he carefully chose the moment to glide back in among the crowd.

Mrs. Gerbati was smoothing down Rosa's hair. "Oh, I

wish they wait. Tomorrow I get you and Salvatore nice warm clothes. I want to show Mamma nice clothes in *fotografia*. Make her so happy. Men always hurry, hurry, hurry. Can't wait. Must do today. Union want to sell lotsa *foto* to make big money to send for strike." She sighed. "They don't think how Mamma need to see children looking warm and happy."

Once again she wrapped her shawl around Rosa. "Tomorrow we get you nice wool coat, and Salvatore brand-new coat, too, yes?"

She was as good as her word. Mr. Gerbati, to Jake's relief, had already left for work when the children got up Monday morning. The kitchen was full of the sweet, yeasty smell of bread baking. He dressed and hurried toward the heavenly aroma. Better than the bakery in the Plains. Besides, it was food that didn't have to be begged or stolen. The Gerbatis had no end of food. They'd had three big meals on Sunday, and the old woman was starting it all over again this morning. It would be hard to leave, he knew. Three meals every day, guaranteed, not to mention a warm bed and the prospect of new clothes.

After she was sure that both Jake and Rosa had eaten their fill and couldn't be persuaded to eat more, Mrs. Gerbati declared that shopping time had come. It was, if anything, colder this morning than it had been yesterday, but the children eagerly followed the old lady out of the house and down the street. She turned when they got to Main, the same street they had paraded up and down on Saturday, and led them into a shop that sold shoes. Only shoes. Shoes of every kind and size.

"First, we get shoes," Mrs. Gerbati declared. "In Vermont you gotta have good shoes for winter, yes?"

"These are a perfect fit for the boy, Mrs. Gerbati," the clerk said, putting a pair of leather boots with thick soles on Jake's feet.

"No, no good," she said.

Jake's heart fell. They were wonderful boots. Too expensive for the old lady, he bet.

"Must get big—see, he grow too fast. Get big size."

"They won't fit nearly so well, Mrs. Gerbati," the clerk protested.

"So? He wear two pair stocking. Must have room to grow."

They went through a similar scene with Rosa, only this time the clerk knew enough to bring big boots the first time. Mrs. Gerbati pulled a tiny black purse out of a pocket in her voluminous black dress, took out a wad of bills, and paid for both pairs.

"Shall I wrap them or—"

"Take off now. We get stocking first, before we wear. We don't want no blister, yes?"

Reluctantly, the children let the clerk take the shining boots off their feet and replace them with their worn-out shoes. But it was the last disappointment of the morning. They went from the shoe store to a store that carried stockings and underwear, as well as a wool dress with ribbons on it for Rosa, a wool suit with long pants and a shirt for Jake, and overcoats for them both. The crowning touch was a cap for Jake and a wool hat for Rosa. At this point, Mrs. Gerbati let them go back into the dressing rooms and put on everything at once while she paid the clerk.

When they met, walking out of their dressing rooms, they could hardly recognize each other. "You look—you look really handsome," Rosa said.

"You don't look so ugly yourself."

"Ah," Mrs. Gerbati said, beaming like the sun above. "*Che bellissimi!* My so beautiful childrens, yes?" She turned toward the clerk for approval.

"Yes, Mrs. Gerbati. They look very nice. I hope they're properly grateful to you and Mr. Gerbati. You've been very generous."

Rosa reddened. They'd been so busy admiring themselves that she'd completely forgotten to say thank you. *"Grazie, Signora Gerbati, grazie."* She gave Sal a stern glare.

"Oh, yeah, thanks, Miz. These are swell."

"Well, that one's a real all-American," the clerk said a bit icily, which caused Rosa to send the boy another one of her looks.

"Yeah, *grazie*." He'd have to watch it. He mustn't be thought of as too all-American. These people seemed to favor Italian kids.

He had warm clothes and better shoes than Mr. Billy Wood, Jake bet. Now all he needed was money for a train ticket. It looked to him that Mrs. Gerbati's purseful of bills was depleted. She'd spent a fortune on the two of them. He was glad, of course, but it meant she probably didn't have much left, not in the purse, anyway. There had to be a stash somewhere. He must keep alert to see where she got her money from. If he hadn't slept so late this morning, he might have spied her filling that little purse. Oh, well, too late for today, but he wouldn't miss his chance again.

The next morning Jake woke in the dark room with a feeling of dread—a hangover from an unremembered dream, perhaps. He lay for a moment listening. Someone was in the toilet next to his room. He could hear the flush and then coughing and wheezing and clearing of a throat. The old man, no doubt of that. From the sound of the clanging of pots from the kitchen, he knew the old lady was up as well. There were no voices, so she must be in there alone. No need to get up. The bed was warm and he had no place to go. Not yet.

He stretched out full length and yawned. No, not time to go back to sleep. Time to think. First he had to figure out where they hid their money. They had money, there was no doubt in Jake's mind about that. He'd seen how she had pulled that wad of bills out of her pocket and peeled them off to pay for the boots *and* all those clothes—*two pairs* of underwear and stockings for each of them—with money left over when she was through. And she hadn't even been expecting two children, just a girl.

Then, abruptly, his mind went back to the shack, waking up there, looking over at Pa so still and peaceful-like, and then, and then. . . .

No. He would not think about that. Nor would he let it scare him into running before he was ready. It would surely be some time before they found him. *They?* Who would even bother to look? It wasn't as though there was anyone in Lawrence who gave a bent penny whether the man lived or died. Jake was his only child—his only relative, even—and Jake had wished him dead more than once. But wishing someone dead was not the same thing as looking over and seeing them dead, realizing you had slept all night with a blinking corpse, not even knowing the man was already stone-cold dead when you got into the bed with him. Warm bed notwithstanding, Jake began to shiver as though he were freezing.

How long had Pa been dead when Jake found him? It had been so cold—it was as though the old man's body had been lying on ice like a great slab of meat. Oh, God, he couldn't stop thinking about it. He had to go some-place far away, where nobody could ever find him. The coppers were bound to ask him questions he didn't want to answer, like how come he hadn't told them when he found his father dead? Or what did he know about his father dying? Oh, God, why hadn't he caught the train to New York City? He should have known which train was which. Besides, there were so many children boarding the New York train, he would have been lost in the shuf-fle—none of this "thirty-five Lawrence children" talk.

Instead of finding his fortune in New York City, here he was in this hick town with an old biddy clucking over him every minute while her sourpuss of a husband was hating his guts for not being his dead son. Not to men-tion a prissy Catholic girl who was always complaining about having to lie and sin because of him.

A knock on the door interrupted his thoughts. "Salvatore. Get-up time. Today is for school."

School? Among all the dangers he'd anticipated, it had never crossed his mind that school would be one of them. How could he go to school? He couldn't even write his real American name, much less the crazy wop one Rosa had given him.

"Are you up? Put on new clothes, yes? And two pair stocking, okay?"

"I don't feel so good," he said in what he imagined was a sickly voice.

"You get up. You eat nice bread and salami, you feel good. Guarantee. Oh, Rosina, you look *bellissima!* Hurry up, Salvatore. You must see your sister. So beautiful."

Jake slid out of bed and went over to the door, which he opened a crack. Rosa, dressed in all her new finery, was looking his way. He crooked his finger and motioned for her to come to the door. With a glance at Mrs. Gerbati's back, she walked over. "Hurry up and get dressed," she said. "Breakfast is ready."

"You got to come in here. I got to talk to you."

"You aren't dressed," she said.

"*Hell's bells.* You can keep your blessed eyes shut. Just come in. I'll get back in bed if it will make you feel better. I got to talk to you."

She closed her eyes until he was safely under the covers and then came in and stood as close to the door as possible.

"Over here. You think I want to yell?"

She took a step in his direction.

"I can't go to school," he said in a loud whisper.

"You got to. Mr. Broggi promised our parents that we'd go to school while we were in Barre."

"Rosa, I can't even write my name. What are they going to think?"

She obviously hadn't thought about that. "Not even your *real* name?"

He shook his head. "I never hardly went to school."

"Oh, dear."

"You got to think of something. You know I can't go."

"*I've* got to think of something? Goodness sakes, Sal, why is it always me that has to think of things?"

"Come on, Rosa, they like you better than they like me. They'll listen to you."

"Are you saying I'm a better liar than you?" She turned to go. "Well, the saints forgive me, I've sure had plenty of practice since I met you." She stomped out, closing the door none too gently behind her.

He could hear the murmur of their voices as she spoke with Mrs. Gerbati. He was tempted to get out of bed and put his ear to the keyhole, but he was afraid of being caught. It might have just been a few minutes but it seemed hours before there was another knock on his door.

"Yeah?"

"Get dressed," Rosa said.

"I can't go—"

"You're not going to school." She opened the door a crack and stuck her head in. "Mrs. Gerbati talked Mr. Gerbati into taking you to work with him."

"*What?*"

"Well, you told me to think of something."

"I didn't tell you to think of *that!*" His whisper was hoarse with anger. The old man hated his guts.

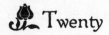 Twenty

Rossi and Gerbati

WELL, WHAT COULD he do? He couldn't stay in bed forever. He got up and put on his new clothes, including the double pair of stockings. Or should he have put on his own clothes? After all, he was going to work with the old man. But it was too late to change. He opened the door and walked into the kitchen. The others were already at the table eating.

"Sit down, Salvatore. Eat up good." Mrs. Gerbati was smiling all over her round face, but Mr. Gerbati was bent over his coffee cup, slurping noisily. He didn't even glance in Jake's direction.

Jake sat down at the empty place. Coffee, black as midnight, was steaming in a mug. There was fresh bread and thick slices of salami on the plate. He might as well eat. He hadn't finished when Mr. Gerbati pushed back his chair and stood up. Jake saw he had on a suit, a shirt, and a ribbon tie. He didn't look like a worker. He looked like Joe Ettor, going out to lead a union rally.

"Mr. Gerbati need to go to shed now, Salvatore. I wrap up your bread, yes?" She got up and took Jake's plate to the counter by the stove. "Put your big coat on. It's cold today."

He got his coat and cap. Mrs. Gerbati handed him his bread, neatly folded up in a napkin. "Put in pocket for later." Then she said something in Italian to Mr. Gerbati, who nodded curtly. Jake looked at Rosa to translate, but she didn't.

"You behave now," she said under her breath. "I told them you wanted to be an apprentice."

He looked at her in disbelief.

"It's that or school," she said sweetly.

Jake followed the old man out the door onto the porch. His new boots crunched on snow blown up from the yard; several more inches had fallen in the night. He plunged his hands into his coat pockets. The fingers of his right hand curled around his napkin-wrapped bread. It was still warm. He stared out toward the street, almost blinded by the brilliant white landscape.

"Come, come," the old man called. "Already I am late."

Jake went carefully down the snow-covered steps and then scurried to catch up, noticing for the first time that Mr. Gerbati was carrying a briefcase. In Jake's experience, only the big shots at the mill carried cases like that. Wasn't Mr. Gerbati a workingman? What was he doing carrying a briefcase? Not that Jake was going to ask. *Hell's bells,* the only thing the man had said to him in two days was to hurry up.

It was a long enough walk from the house to Mr. Gerbati's shed to freeze his nose and the tips of his ears peeping out from under his new cap. The boots were wonderful, though. His feet were as warm as they'd been under the quilt in bed. Now, if only he had something to cover his face and his hands, he'd be able to stand the cruelest weather.

The old man could walk amazingly fast. He seemed to be paying no attention at all to Jake. *If he don't care whether I live or die, how come he agreed to let me go to work with him? He wants something out of me, most like. Well, I want something out of him, too. And I bet I get mine first.*

They went down the hill past a school, the one he was escaping, no doubt, and on to Main Street. There they turned left, walked a block or two, and turned right for a couple of blocks until they came to a series of long shedlike frame buildings with a branch of the railroad track running into each one.

"Is here," Mr. Gerbati said, going down the length of one of the smaller sheds, past huge bolted double doors with a large sign above them that announced, Jake could only guess, the names of the owners. The track ran underneath the doors. Jake followed Mr. Gerbati around the shed to a small door toward the back corner of the building. Here the old man took out his watch fob. With the key that was hanging from it, he unlocked the door, then pushed it open and nodded for Jake to go in. The shed was a large, high-ceilinged area. To the right of the door, in the corner, was a smaller windowed room. There was no one inside the building. Count on the old man to be the first guy to show up for work. In the dry, dusty light, the room looked to Jake almost like a mill floor, except that instead of rows of spindles or looms, there were large blocks of granite sitting around here and there, and, at the far end to the left, some kind of massive machinery.

Mr. Gerbati turned a switch, and electric lights hanging from the ceiling brightened the area. Then he went into the small room in the corner and turned on the light in there. It was an office. Through the window Jake could see the old man hanging his coat on a peg and putting on a large tan-colored apron. That might explain the briefcase. He worked in the office, not as a laborer as Jake had thought. After all, the man did have his own house.

Suddenly, his ears were pierced by the high pitch of a factory whistle, then others, as though the whole town were exploding into whistles. Mr. Gerbati went to the door and opened it wide, letting in a blast of winter wind. Before long, men began to come piling through. *"Buon giorno, Signor Gerbati."* Mr. Gerbati nodded and smiled and murmured a greeting to each man as he came in. Most of them took notice of Jake with a smile or a greeting. But there was no loitering. The men headed for a line of pegs against the wall and exchanged their overcoats for large aprons like the one Mr. Gerbati had put on. Most of the men kept their caps on, but a few exchanged their caps for little paper hats that seemed to have been folded out of newspaper.

The men scattered then, some toward the end of the room where the machinery stood, others to various stations around the room where there were a few statues of angels and what Jake figured to be saints. But most of the men went to what appeared to be tombstones in various stages of completion. Jake swallowed. He didn't want to spend his days in a place that looked like a fancy graveyard, surrounded by reminders of death.

But no one else seemed to mind, and soon they were all busy at work. Some of the men used powered drills; others carefully chipped away at the rock with hammers and chisels. He counted eight men in this part of the shed—nine if you included Mr. Gerbati. Four or five had gone to the other end, from which he could hear the noise of massive machinery starting up. Only Mr. Gerbati had gone into the office. There he was, sitting at a desk. Jake had to conclude that Mr. Gerbati was the overseer of this shed.

So what was Jake supposed to do? Stand there by the door like a dummy in his new boots and overcoat? The floor was covered with stone chips. He was glad for his thick-soled boots. The air was quickly filling with dust. Just like the mill but worse, somehow. This dust had a bite to it. Jake coughed to clear his throat. Mr. Gerbati, just as though he could hear Jake's cough over the noise of drilling and pounding of the machinery, got up from his desk and came to the door of the little office. He looked about the shed, then walked over to where a large man with a freckled face and a mustache the color of rusty pipe was working. Mr. Gerbati said something to him. The man looked toward Jake and nodded. Mr. Gerbati, apparently satisfied, went back into the office.

"I understand you're one of the Lawrence boys," the man said, coming over to where Jake stood and putting out a dusty hand for him to shake. "I'm Duncan, and you're . . . ?"

"Sal," Jake said.

"Welcome to Rossi and Gerbati's, Sal."

"Gerbati is one of the *owners?*"

"Mr. Gerbati is *the* owner. Old Mr. Rossi died last year from—well, we call it 'stonecutter's TB.'" Duncan laughed. "It's likely to get us all in the end, but meanwhile. . . . Hey, hang your coat on a peg and then come over and make yourself at home. You might want to leave your cap on—the dust, you know." He started back toward the stone he'd been working on.

Jake hung up his coat and went to Duncan's station,

still puzzling over what the man had said. *Owner?* Owners were like Mr. Billy Wood. But there were small owners, too, weren't there, like the baker and the grocer? Well, it was a small shed, not as large as several they'd passed on the way here or the great horseshoe buildings he had seen from the train window.

"Yeah, Mr. Gerbati is the best boss I ever had, including my own father. We start coughing, and home we go to rest up. But I'd work for Mr. Gerbati even if he was mean as old man Rossi, because he's one of the greatest artists this side of the Atlantic."

"Artist?"

"Yeah, look here, Sal." He pointed to the stone he'd been working on. "See these roses?"

Jake looked, and out of the gray of the granite flowers were blooming. They were as delicate as the real thing, which he'd only seen once over the fence in a rich man's summer garden. But here they were in stone, every petal fresh and alive. "Mr. Gerbati did those?"

"He's a genius with flowers—roses, lilies, daisies, daffodils, morning glories, pansies. . . . He can even do a perfect thistle for us Scots. He's a genius, he is."

"I didn't know."

"No, I'm sure he wouldn't have told you. He's as humble as Rossi was arrogant. But every one of us is here because we want to learn from him."

Duncan was chipping at the stone to carve a name.

"Hey, would you hand me that point?" He indicated a sharp chisel lying on the stone near where Jake was standing. "Yeah, we call them points, and this"—he raised his mallet—"is a hammer. I'll try to teach you what we call our tools as we go along." He took the point that Jake handed him and began to work again. It was a tombstone, no question about that, but with Mr. Gerbati's roses blooming on it, more beautiful than any stone Jake would ever have seen or imagined.

"Mr. Gerbati wants me to keep you busy," Duncan said, carefully holding his point in place as he spoke, "but I've never had an assistant, so I'm not sure what you ought to be doing. You could sit down and watch, if you like. Pull up a slab and make yourself comfortable."

Oh, he was joking. Jake smiled to show he'd understood, and perched himself on a block of granite nearby. Duncan grinned and went back to his task.

He didn't know how long he'd sat on the granite, but he knew the cold of the stone had overcome even the warmth of his new wool trousers. He stood up and wiggled to restore circulation in his seat. Mr. Gerbati saw him, came to the office door, and beckoned him over. Jake told himself that he wasn't afraid of the old man. Hadn't Duncan just sung his praises? But he couldn't help being nervous. What did the old man want of him?

"Here," Mr. Gerbati said, handing Jake an empty bucket. "The shovel over there, by the door—you see?

You clean the grout off the floor. Duncan will show you where to dump it."

That was all, a job to do. "Yes, sir," he said, so relieved that he almost smiled at the old fellow.

Duncan took time from his chiseling to explain that "grout" was all the chips of granite on the floor. "Don't try to fill the bucket—you'll never be able to lift it. And just go to where no one is working. They won't want to stop for you to shovel."

So he had a job after all. Not a very grand one. He shoveled up granite chips and carried them out the door to a pile of stone near the creek. It was hard work—even partially full, the bucket was heavy—but he didn't mind. The men were friendly, and no one yelled at him to hurry or cursed him if he accidentally got in the way.

"Does the train really come in here?" he asked Duncan. The idea of a train coming right into the shed excited him.

"Not in winter," Duncan said. "It's too cold to quarry now. They'll bring our blocks down from the hill when the weather's warmer."

It was a disappointment, but the crane almost made up for it. He watched, his mouth open, as two men down by the machinery put a heavy chain belt around each end of a block of granite. It was raised up off the floor by another chain attached to a metal bar that went across the shed near the ceiling, and then the bar started down a track, carrying the immense stone the length of the room to a stonecutter's station. The first time Jake saw it, he ducked. But there was a man following behind the granite, making sure it didn't swing out and hit anything or anybody. No one else was worried about the stone falling or hitting him, so Jake wasn't scared exactly, but he felt a little thrill of fear every time he heard the movement of the crane over the noise of the shed, and looked up to see the stone riding above them.

At what he later learned was 11 A.M., the whistles wheezed and shrieked once more. "Dinnertime," Duncan announced. The men knocked the dust off their clothes, hung up their aprons, put on their coats, and hurried out. Jake got his coat and waited by the door for Mr. Gerbati. Dinnertime! And there was a warm place to go and food would be there waiting, he knew. What difference did it make if the old man hated him? His pa (he could never suppress the pang that name caused) had beat him. Mr. Gerbati had only yelled. It was a poor fool of a fellow who couldn't take a bit of screaming.

When they reached the house, a red-faced Mrs. Gerbati met them at the door. They had hardly got in the house before she began sputtering. "You don't want to go home, do you, Salvatore? You like it here, *si?*"

"Yeah, yeah, I like it fine." What was the matter with the old lady? She looked as though she was about to burst into tears.

"The mamma and papa of two of our Lawrence boys say they want the boys home. They say in telegram that papa no give permission. We take—we steal—what you say?"

"Kidnap?"

"*Si*, kidanapa their boys. But we don't, no? Your papa want you to come, yes, Salvatore?"

"My pa is dead." He watched her eyes shift. What did she suspect?

"*Si, si, scusami.* I forget. My heart all upset. Mamma sign card, yes? She want you to come to Barre?"

"Uh, yeah. She signed."

Mrs. Gerbati leaned toward him conspiratorily. "We don't tell Rosa, no? She so homesick for Mamma. Don't tell her Colonni boys go home tomorrow, okay?"

He nodded. Rosa would find out, he knew, but he wasn't going to be the one to tell her.

"And we don't *make* you go to work in the shed, yes?"

"No. I mean, yes, no one made me go."

"We promise, you see, we send all childrens to school, don't make them work."

"But I wanted to work."

"That's what I say to Mr. Broggi. You say you *want* to go with Mr. Gerbati. No go school."

"They ain't going to make me go to school, are they?"

"I don't know. They don't like you go to shed. Not so

healthy, they say, for growing boy." She glanced toward the front window. "Shh. Hush. She coming."

By the time Rosa got in the house, Mrs. Gerbati had taken herself to the kitchen. "Come, come, eat! *Zuppa* get cold. No good."

They gathered around the kitchen table. Rosa's hair had been freshly plaited with red ribbons tied to either braid. Her cheeks were still pink from the cold, and her eyes were shining. School seemed to agree with her.

"Is good school on Brook Street?"

"Yes. They even lent me some books to bring home."

"You gotta good teacher?"

"She's very nice. Miss Moulton."

"You grow up to be teacher, Rosa. We needa good teachers for Italian childrens."

It seemed obvious that Rosa hadn't heard about the boys going home. But she would by tonight. Then he'd be in a pickle. If she demanded to go, he was likely to be sent home with her. But if she stayed, they might force him to go to school, and then the jig would be up, for sure.

Mr. Gerbati finished slurping in the last of his coffee and scraped his chair back.

"Oh, so soon! *Scusami*, Salvatore. Mr. Gerbati always first back from *colazione*." She made an attempt to whistle with her mouth. "Got to pull the—the, you know—"

Jake jumped up. He wasn't going to let the old man leave him behind.

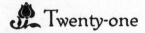 Twenty-one

Word from Home

WHEN ROSA RETURNED to school after the midday meal, she was immediately greeted by one of the other Lawrence children. "Did you hear about the Colonni boys?" and when Rosa said she hadn't, the story began to pour out. She could tell that Tony had mixed up several versions in his excitement, but the main point was clear. The Colonni brothers' father said that he had not given permission for his sons to come to Vermont, that they had gotten on board the train instead of some other children. All the Barre people were swearing that they had been told that every child had had the proper permission card signed. Perhaps, in the confusion, some child might have boarded by mistake, but they could hardly believe that two children could have escaped their notice.

Rosa listened in horror. She knew perfectly well that Sal had no permission card and that he had boarded and passed almost unnoticed. But if a mistake had been made with these two boys, the Barre committee would be on the alert for other mistakes. She needed to warn him, but there was no way to do so before that night.

Tony, who was telling her breathlessly about the case, wound up by saying, "And they don't want to go home at all. They got plenty to eat and warm clothes. They like it here. It's a vacation, just like the union promised."

"They don't want to go home?"

"No. They're mad as wet cats."

Oh, if it had only been Rosa, not these silly boys, who was leaving tomorrow. Then she'd be home and she wouldn't have to worry about Mamma and Anna and Ricci anymore, much less Sal and all his problems and lies. It was hardly fair. Boys who didn't want to leave having to go, while she, who wanted so much to go home, must stay. Not only stay, but dream up more lies to help that wretched boy, whose real name and story she didn't even know, except that there was something dark, some shadow he was running away from. Of course, she was curious—anyone would be—but she was also terrified that he might tell her everything, and then she'd have the burden of even more lies as well as some wicked secret to keep hidden.

When she came in from school, she found Sal in the kitchen stuffing his mouth with bread and cheese. She made him leave his snack on the table and come into the hall with her.

"Can't it wait?" he asked grumpily. "I'm eating."

"They're sending two of the boys home to Lawrence tomorrow."

"Oh, yeah," he said, already turning to go back into the kitchen. "I heard already."

"You don't understand." She grabbed his arm. "They'll be checking on *everyone* now. They think there may have been a mixup boarding the train. . . ."

"Yeah?" He was trying to act nonchalant, but she could tell he was worried.

"Well, what are we going to do?"

"Nothing. I told you I'd be leaving soon."

"But if you run away now, I'm the one who'll have to explain why."

He gave her a wry grin. "You're getting good at explaining. You'll think of something."

He was infuriating. "I have a good mind to march right into that kitchen this minute and tell Mrs. Gerbati everything!"

Alarm crossed his face, but he controlled it. "You wouldn't do that."

"And just why wouldn't I?"

"Because you're in too deep, that's why."

She knew he was right. The Gerbatis trusted her. They wouldn't understand if she suddenly announced that all she had said about Sal had been lies.

"You can tell them one thing, though."

"And what is that?"

"The real reason I can't go to school."

"I thought you'd be too ashamed."

"It'll be worse if they make me go."

She stared at him. He was ashamed—really ashamed—of not being able to read or write even his own name. She wanted to say, *I'll teach you*, but that might make matters worse.

"Mr. Marchesi come by to tell Mrs. Gerbati I was supposed to be in school, not working. Part of the deal was that the people here would send all the kids to school, not make them work."

"Nobody's making you work, are they?"

"No. I kinda like it. It's not near as hard as the mill. And all the guys are friendly to me. Even the old·man ain't too bad."

"Okay," she said finally. "I'll tell them, but I may have to tell the truth."

He reddened, but he nodded. "Whatever you have to do. I can't go to no school."

Rosa went to Mr. Gerbati, who had fetched his afternoon newspaper from the market around the corner and was reading in the sitting room while his wife finished putting supper on the table. "Sal asked me to talk to you, Mr. Gerbati," she began.

He folded the paper on his lap and looked at her over his little metal-rimmed glasses. "He can't talk for himself?"

"He's too ashamed."

"So?"

She took a deep breath. "Sal can't go to school, Mr. Gerbati. He—he's never been, so he would have to start with the little ones. He's too ashamed to be in the first grade with six- and seven-year-olds."

Mr. Gerbati was waiting for her to go on.

"I know it seems strange . . . me going to school and my brother not. But—but he was, well, when he was six, he was very sick, and when he got well again, he refused to go. You may have noticed that he's very stubborn." Mr. Gerbati gave a faint smile. "So finally Papa paid the man for the papers, and Sal went to work in the mill. He was as big as some of the older boys, and nobody asks questions at the mill anyway. Besides, we needed the money. Then Papa was killed, and we needed it even worse."

"So, if he's worker, why is he here with children?"

"I—I wouldn't come alone. I was too scared. There was no work with the strike going, and," she put on her saddest face, "he was hungry, too."

Mr. Gerbati ran his finger along the crease of his paper. "When Mr. Broggi go to Lawrence, he promise all the children go to school. Mr. Marchesi tell Mrs. Gerbati today, all the committee know Sal no go to school."

"I know. But you could explain to Mr. Marchesi and Mr. Broggi. Mamma would understand. She won't expect

Sal to be in school, only that he behave himself and help you any way he can. We're both so grateful to you and Mrs. Gerbati. . . ."

"Tell your brother next time he speak for himself, *si?* Not send little sister." He turned back to his paper.

At supper neither of the Gerbatis mentioned the return of the Colonni brothers to Lawrence, nor the visit Mr. Marchesi had paid to check on their charges. But after the old man had finished the last of his wine and his coffee, into which Rosa noticed he poured a bit of grappa from a jug on the counter, he pushed back his chair and addressed Sal. "Your sister say you like work in the shed better than school, yes?"

"Yessir," Sal murmured to his empty plate.

"You work hard, you behave good, I fix with committee, okay?"

"Thank you, sir," Sal said without lifting his head. *"Grazie."*

"But after work, you gotta study, *si?* Rosa, she smart girl, she teach you. And I don't want no monkey business, neither. You study good. You go home after strike and you no dumb kid, okay?"

"Yessir."

"Begin tonight. I tell Mr. Broggi and Mr. Marchesi you study at Gerbatis' house, okay?"

So it was all right, at least for now. She'd gotten the wretched boy through one more scrape. It would be nice to think he was grateful, but she doubted it. She began that night at the kitchen table writing "Salvatore Serutti" in big curling letters at the top of the paper that Mrs. Gerbati had found for her. Then below she wrote the alphabet, first in capitals, then in lowercase. "Now copy everything," she ordered, "while I study my own lessons."

He was sweating, holding the pencil tightly in his right fist. She knew he would have objected if the Gerbatis hadn't been in the next room, Mrs. Gerbati smiling with pride over her two charges working away on their lessons at the kitchen table.

Mr. Broggi escorted the Colonni boys to Lawrence the next day on the afternoon train. The word came back that their mother wept with regret when she saw her sons so well dressed. The mill owners' agents had lied to the parents, had pressured them to demand the boys' return, saying that they were being harshly treated in Vermont, that they were no more than slaves to the rough and drunken stonecutters in that godforsaken place. When the boys told them about the parade and the feast at the Labor Hall and how every meal since had been a feast, even the father begged Mr. Broggi's forgiveness. Maybe more children should go to this paradise in the north, the Colonnis said.

Thursday, Mr. Broggi returned. All the children at

school were hoping for word from home. So as soon as the dismissal bell rang, Rosa raced back to the Gerbatis', past Mr. Gerbati reading his paper, and into the kitchen, where Mrs. Gerbati had evidently just given Sal a fat slice of bread slathered with butter to "hold his belly" until supper was ready.

"Did my mamma send any word by Mr. Broggi?" Rosa asked by way of greeting.

Mrs. Gerbati smiled and pulled a folded piece of paper from her apron pocket. "She write to Rosa," she explained to Sal. "You learn good to read, she write you, too, yes?"

Rosa unfolded the paper. It had been written not by Mamma, but by Anna. Mamma couldn't write well in Italian, much less in English.

> Dear Rosa,
> How are you doing in Barry, Vermont? We miss you, but Mr. Broggi says all the children ther are doing fine and we must not lisen to lies from the mill people. Ther are a lot of lies about Lawrence children being kidnaped and carried away to New York and Vermont, but Mamma says we know they are lies, jus like the other lies we been told.

Mamma meens to send me and Ricci to Filadelfia on Saturday. I don't want to go, but Ricci is to yung to go alone and I have been coffing more and Mamma says I need to go where I can get good food and a warm place to stay.

We got the post card you sent and also the pitchur of you and a boy from Mr. Broggi. Who is that boy? You look good, but his fase was blury. Mamma thought Mr. Broggi said something about her son, but Mamma must have got it wrong. I worry the masheens have made her def like Mrs. Marino. By the way Mrs. Marino has been to jail. She hit a milisha with a pot of slop from her window. They let her go tho. I think Mrs. Marino is to much troble even for the polees. Rite soon.

Love,
Anna

I forgot to say. Olga Kronsky say to tell you Miss Finch bring breakfast for class every day now.

A large tear rolled down her cheek and plopped down on "Filadelfia," making it a smear.

"Bad news, Rosina?"

"No, Mrs. Gerbati. Just . . . Mamma is sending my sister and baby brother to Philadelphia on Saturday."

"Aw, Philadelphia. We want more children in Barre. Why go to Philadelphia? Too big city. Barre nice, lotsa nice Italian family here."

She sounded so much like Mamma that it was all Rosa could do to keep from bursting into tears.

"You don't read your mamma's letter to your brother?" Mr. Gerbati was standing at the kitchen door. "Or don't he care for news from home?"

"Oh, yes, sure, of course he cares. I'm sorry, Sal."

Sal looked up from his plate. Mrs. Gerbati had given him a second slice of bread and butter, so he hadn't been paying any attention to the old woman and Rosa. "Huh?"

"It's a letter from Mamma."

"Yeah?"

"Our big sister Anna and our little brother Ricci are going to Philadelphia on Saturday." She realized, a bit late, that it sounded as though she was talking to a dimwit. After all, Sal ought to know who Anna and Ricci were.

"Yeah? That's nice."

"And Mrs. Marino had to go to jail. She—uh—poured—uh—slop from her window on a Harvard boy's head."

"Yeah?" Sal laughed out loud. "Good for her. That would mess up a pretty uniform."

"They—they took her to jail, but Anna says they didn't keep her long. You know Mrs. Marino. Like Anna says, she was probably too much trouble even for the police."

Mrs. Gerbati was looking a bit shocked, but Sal was thoroughly enjoying this bit of news.

"And, of course, everyone sends you their love."

He actually blushed when she said that. Probably it was the first time anyone anywhere had ever sent him love. It was too bad it was just another of her lies.

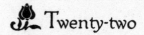 Twenty-two

Tumulto and Treachery

SATURDAY CAME. It was the day Anna and Ricci would be going to Philadelphia and leaving Mamma behind with only the Jarusalises for comfort. Rosa went with Mrs. Gerbati to confession where Rosa admitted to telling a number of vague untruths. She didn't venture to be too specific. The priest didn't press her, but gave her the usual Hail Marys and Our Fathers to recite, and they were back, preparing for supper, when the telephone rang. There was a large contraption of wood and metal and wires attached to the wall in the front hall, which Mrs. Gerbati had proudly pointed out to be a telephone. Rosa had never seen anyone using it, and it took her a minute to realize that the ringing noise she heard was inside, rather than outside, the house.

"Ah, *il telefono*," Mrs. Gerbati exclaimed, wiping her hands on her apron and hurrying into the hall to pick it up. Rosa couldn't help it—she followed Mrs. Gerbati right out the kitchen door. She'd never known anyone actually to talk on a telephone, and she was curious to see how it worked.

"'Ello, 'ello?" Mrs. Gerbati had pulled part of the instrument from the wall and cupped it over her right ear. She was standing on tiptoe, yelling into a sort of raised ring on the front. "*Si, si.*" And from then on she was mostly yelling *Si* or breathing a hushed *No* into the instrument. The only thing Rosa was sure of was that the news from the other end was not good. She could read that much from the growing expression of alarm on Mrs. Gerbati's face.

As soon as Mrs. Gerbati replaced the earpiece, Rosa called out to her, "What is it? What's the matter?"

Mrs. Gerbati took her by the hand and led her back into the warm kitchen. "Sit, Rosina."

Rosa obeyed. Mrs. Gerbati sat in the chair beside her, still holding her hand and shaking her head. Suddenly, as though something had just occurred to her, she raised her head and looked about. "Where is Salvatore?"

"I don't know. He said he was going out for a walk after he had his snack. I think he likes to wander around town. He'll be back soon, but you don't need to wait for him. . . ."

"Better we wait for him." She let go of Rosa's hand and patted her knee. "And Mr. Gerbati, too, yes?" Mr. Gerbati had gone to the Labor Hall. He might not even come home for supper.

"Is it about Mamma?"

"Don't worry, *bambina*. Is all right, all good. You see."

Rosa didn't see anything at all except that nothing was good. Something terrible had happened to Mamma, that was it. Something so terrible that the news had to come by telephone, not telegram or letter. News so terrible that Mrs. Gerbati didn't even dare to tell her. Rosa was shaking all over, despite her warm clothes, despite the warm kitchen. Couldn't Mrs. Gerbati see what she was doing to her? Torturing her with silence? But Mrs. Gerbati had gotten up and gone to the kitchen counter. She took the leftover polenta from the night before, now congealed, and sliced it with a piece of string. She put the neat slices into a cast-iron pan sizzling with olive oil and began to fry them, concentrating on the task as if her life depended on it. If Rosa had thought it would do any good, she would have thrown herself at the old woman's feet and begged her to tell, but she knew Mrs. Gerbati was determined to make her husband the teller of bad news—news so terrible that she could not bring herself to break it.

Finally, Sal came back and, minutes later, Mr. Gerbati. It might as well have been days, as far as Rosa was concerned, for by the time the old man opened the door, Rosa had mentally gone to the DeCesare funeral parlor and seen the bodies of her loved ones laid out like

Annie Lopizzo, and then followed the hearse that carried her entire family to paupers' graves in the Lawrence cemetery. Or would the union pay for a proper burial? They ought to. They were at fault. If it hadn't been for the union, she would still have a family.

"Some coffee and bread?" Mrs. Gerbati asked a bit too chirpily as her husband and Sal entered the kitchen. "To comfort the belly after your cold walk?" Both Sal and Mr. Gerbati sat down at the table while she served them. "And you, Rosa?"

Rosa shook her head, unable to speak. She was numb with terrified anticipation. Mrs. Gerbati was sending silent signals to Mr. Gerbati across Sal's head, but the boy seemed to notice nothing but his food. Finally, Mr. Gerbati cleared his throat.

"I hear at the Labor Hall some news," he began. Rosa looked up quickly. Sal kept munching away on his bread. "There was a—a *tumulto* at the station. . . ."

"What station?" Rosa blurted out.

"In Lawrence. The parents was taking their children to the train."

"To go to Philadelphia?" Rosa could not help herself. She had to know. Why couldn't he go ahead and tell her if Mamma and Anna and Ricci were dead or alive? They must be dead—why else all the delay?

He nodded. "To Philadelphia," he said. "The police—"

"Mamma's dead."

Both Mr. and Mrs.Gerbati started in alarm. "*No! No!*" They chorused.

"*Povera bambina!*" Mrs. Gerbati came from the stove and put her arms around Rosa, crushing the girl's face to her wide bosom. "*No, no,* don't I tell you no worry? Is all right? You tell Rosa is all right," she commanded her husband.

"The police attack the people," Mr. Gerbati continued. "No dead, but some beat with police stick. We don't know 'bout your mamma and sister"—he glanced at Sal, who was still chewing his food—"if hurt or not. We only know Mamma and sister in jail and baby boy took away to somewhere we don't know."

Rosa let out a cry, which prompted Mrs. Gerbati to hug her closer.

"Mr. Broggi, he in touch with union committee in Lawrence. He get more news, he telephone, okay?"

"Why do they do such terrible thing, Mr. Gerbati?" Mrs. Gerbati sounded near to tears herself. "Beat up womens and little childrens and snatch baby away from Mamma? What kind of people do such terrible thing?"

"Only people who fear. Fear make people crazy."

"What have they got to be scared of?" Sal said. He'd stopped chewing and begun to pay attention at last. "They got all the guns."

"Guns don't win this kinda war," Mr. Gerbati said, thumping his chest. "Is heart. Is strong in here."

🐝   🐝   🐝

Rosa could hardly eat, and later it was even harder to sleep. Pictures of Mamma and Anna in what she imagined to be the Lawrence jail filled her mind. And little Ricci. Where was he? She couldn't even imagine what must have happened to her poor baby brother. It would be better for him to be in jail, wouldn't it? At least he would be with Mamma and Anna, not carried away by strangers. She was, by turn, hot with anger and cold with fear. Why had she left them? She could have kept them out of trouble if she'd been there. No, probably not. Mamma was a hardheaded Italian woman after all. Well, then . . . she would have been in jail with them. Wasn't that better than being here all safe and warm and well fed while everyone she loved was suffering? She began to cry again, quietly into her pillow, so as not to disturb the Gerbatis in the next room.

Morning came at last. Rosa dressed and went into the kitchen. Some morning, she promised herself, she'd get up before Mrs. Gerbati, surprise her by starting the fire in the stove. Not today, however. Mrs. Gerbati had the stove roaring and coffee bubbling on the back of it. The bread for the day had risen and was already baking in the hot oven. She gave Rosa a big smile, though her eyes were pained as they searched the girl's face. "You sleep okay?"

Rosa shrugged in answer.

"Me, too." The woman sighed. "So much worry for Mamma and sister and baby. But it be all right, yes? We get good news soon, you see. Mr. Broggi find out soon, fix everything."

"I got to go home, Mrs. Gerbati."

"No! You can't go. Your mamma not even there."

"The Jarusalises—the people who live in our apartment—they are there—at least Granny will be. She won't be in jail. I have to go and find out about Mamma and Anna, and especially Ricci. I don't even know where Ricci is! He'll be scared to death. He doesn't like strangers at all. He won't know what happened to him."

"Shh, shh. Hush. We talk to Mr. Broggi. We find out everything soon, yes? Now, come to Mass like good girl and we pray to Virgin, okay? We light special candle—one for Mamma, one for Anna, and one for baby Ricci, yes?"

What else could she do? She had no money for train fare. She fetched her coat and hat and put them on. Mrs. Gerbati hung up her apron and threw her great wool shawl over her head and wrapped it around her shoulders.

"Salvatore not go, yes?"

Rosa shook her head. He was probably sleeping like a baby. He wasn't worried about anything.

She couldn't know that at that moment Jake was lying in his bed, staring at the ceiling. It was all going to explode soon. The police had arrested Rosa's ma. There would be questions, if not from the police, from the stinking union committee. It wouldn't be more than a day or so before . . . He was actually sweating. It was a cold sweat but sweat nonetheless. He had to get that money today before everything blew sky high. There was a safe in the office. He had seen customers come to the office and give Mr. Gerbati money, which he had locked up in a little metal safe under his desk once they were gone. The key was on Mr. Gerbati's watch fob. Not much chance of pinching that. But how tough could that lock be? With one of their precious points and a hammer, couldn't he jimmy it? Make it look like a robbery? Well, it wouldn't matter if they suspected him. He'd be long gone before Mr. Gerbati discovered the broken lock and missing cash.

He began to sweat again. The police of two towns would be after him. But how smart could the police in a hick town like this be, anyway? Besides, he'd gotten the distinct impression from the men at work that the police didn't have much use for the Italian community. Too much drinking and brawling and loud talk in the streets. Duncan had said even his own family, being Scots, hated it that he was working in a wop shed. Duncan had really said "Eye-talian" not "wop." They wouldn't have minded so much if the shed had been owned by a Scot. Duncan's pa had come from Scotland to get the granite out of the ground. Now all the men in Duncan's family, except for him, worked in the quarries.

Duncan would despise him if he stole the money and ran. But why should he care what Duncan thought? The man actually thought old man Gerbati was a kind of god, creating living things out of dead rock.

What if he didn't run? Not at first anyway. If he stole the money and hid it and waited a day or two, then they wouldn't suspect him. If he grabbed it and ran, of course they'd be after him like a shot. Mr. Gerbati would send every goon in the labor union after him. And Rosa, tired of lying for him, would squeal that he'd taken the first train to New York. Then he'd have every cop in New York City on his tail.

He sat up in bed. Today was the day to do it. Nobody went near the sheds on a Sunday. It would be Monday morning before the theft was discovered, and he'd be there, shoveling up the grout, innocent as a daisy. Creeping to his door, he listened while Rosa and the old woman left for church. He dressed quickly, then waited silently until he heard the old man's feet on the stairs. He was headed for the bathroom at the end of the down-stairs hall. The door shut, and then Jake could hear the regular morning noises of the old man. First there was the rush of the flushing toilet, then raspy coughing and wheezing and clearing of the throat, a morning ritual before he shaved his face. He waited until he heard

Gerbati in the hall, putting on his overcoat. He was getting ready to go fetch his morning newspaper. The front door opened. . . . It was safe to leave. By the time the old man turned the corner and started uphill for the shop, Jake would be out the kitchen door, heading downhill to the shed.

The sky was gray; the sun had yet to make its way through the heavy clouds, which might or might not mean more snow before the day was over. Jake could tell it had snowed during the night. It seemed to snow all the time up here. He was tired of snow. Oh, it was pretty all right, like now when it first came down, but run a few horses and wagons through it, not to mention automobiles, and it churned up as bad as the slush in the Lawrence streets. Well, no matter. He wasn't out for sightseeing today.

He felt a tickle of excitement in his chest. This was better than going after a poor box. This was the real thing. He quickened his steps. There were not many people on the streets in the North End. The pious were in church. The others were sleeping off the effects of Saturday night. Why, by the time he got to the shed, even the old man would be home, settled in his chair, his glasses on his nose, reading his infernal Italian newspaper. He crossed Main Street without seeing a single vehicle, not even a trolley car. What a dead burg this was!

Just in case, just in case anyone happened to notice him—and he always felt conspicuous in his grand overcoat—he turned off Main Street a block before he needed to and wound his way in and out of sheds before he approached Rossi and Gerbati. How was he going to get in? He'd forgotten that the outside door also had a lock. Never mind, he'd broken into plenty of places before. He forced the small window in the office up far enough to let him wriggle through and slide headfirst onto the office floor. The room was dark, but he wasn't going to risk turning on any lights.

He pulled down the window and went over to examine the safe. He knelt down and ran his thumb along the edge, trying to measure the width of a cutter's point that might fit in the crack between the door and the wall of the little metal safe. The whole thing looked flimsy.

Now to find the right tool. For this he went into the shed proper. Mr. Gerbati always took his own precious tools home with him, but not all the cutters were so fussy. Duncan had left a hammer and several points on the granite block beside his monument. Jake put out his hand, but something made him draw it back. He'd get some other fellow's tools, not Duncan's. He might chip them, and Duncan was pretty particular.

It was harder to find the right point than he'd imagined. The shed was dark, and even when he'd take one over to the window to examine it, it was hard to tell. He took several into the office, only to have to return them as too wide for the crack, which seemed to grow narrower each time he tried to insert a point.

After what felt like an eternity, he found a point sharp enough to slide into the miserable crack. He stood up and took off his overcoat and threw it over Mr. Gerbati's chair. He was sweating again and breathing too fast. He coughed—the wretched air was clogged with dust even on a Sunday. He knelt again in front of the safe and jammed the point into the crack right at the place where the door lock met the wall. He picked up the hammer. *Hell's bells,* it was heavy, and his hand was shaking like a leaf in a windstorm. He raised it and struck the first blow with all his might. Nothing. He struck again. Nothing seemed to be giving. Now sweat was running down from his hair and stinging his eyes, but he didn't have to see to strike. *Clang! Clang!* They could probably hear the racket from Main Street. But he couldn't stop now. He raised the hammer and attacked the end of the point over and over again, lifting his right arm high. . . .

Something caught his wrist in the air, twisting it so that the hammer clanked heavily to the floor. Terrified, he wrenched his neck to see that it was little Mr. Gerbati above him, his veined hand gripping Jake's wrist like an iron vise.

Twenty-three

The Bargain

Mr. GERBATI LET GO of Jake's wrist, leaned over, and picked up the hammer and the point, now badly blunted. He put them carefully on the table. Then he took Jake's overcoat off his desk chair. "Up to your feet," he said. "We go." He handed Jake the overcoat and waited for him to put it on.

At both the office and the outside doors, Mr. Gerbati stepped aside for Jake to go through first. And then, as though he had no fear of what Jake might do, he turned his back on the boy and carefully locked the shed door.

Should he try to make a break for it? But where could he go? Where could he hide? Jake felt paralyzed. He just stood outside in the snow and waited for what the old man was going to say. How had Gerbati known? He'd sneaked into the office without Jake realizing it because Jake had been so intent on jimmying the infernal lock, making so much racket of his own. But how had the old man known where Jake would be, what he'd planned to do? Why had Gerbati suddenly taken a notion on a Sunday morning to come to the shed? It was all too neat, as if God had put it in the old man's mind to catch him.

Mr. Gerbati returned his watch fob to his vest pocket, buttoned his suit coat, then his overcoat, and started to walk, but he was not taking the usual route home. He was following two sets of footprints in the snow around several long neighboring sheds before heading over to Main Street, which was still pristine with blinding new snow—except for the same two pairs of footprints. As though taunting Jake, Mr. Gerbati followed the tracks like a bloodhound in reverse right up to his own back door and into his kitchen, where Mrs. Gerbati was bustling about laying out her usual bountiful Sunday morning spread.

"We took walk," Mr. Gerbati said, as though an explanation were required.

It was a late breakfast, as it would be on a Sunday following Mass. Rosa hardly touched her food. Still mooning over her stupid family, Jake supposed. The girl didn't know what real trouble was. He was sure he wouldn't be able to eat, either—his belly seemed to have taken up residence in his throat—but when Mrs. Gerbati said, "Eat, eat," he obeyed. He found, to his amazement, that the food went down the usual way and stayed there.

Mr. Gerbati got up as soon as he had finished his coffee spiked with the spirits he always liked to slop into the cup at the end of a meal. He went into the hall, shutting the kitchen door behind him. They could hear him talking out there, the words muffled but apparently in English.

"*Telefonata*—call on telephone," Mrs. Gerbati explained.

Telephone call? Gerbati must be calling the police . . . or worse. Now the rich, oily meal did threaten to rise from his stomach. Jake wanted to make some excuse to get out of there—to go to his room or to the toilet—but he sat frozen, trying to hear through the wall what Mr. Gerbati might be saying into that infernal machine.

"Get your coat, Salvatore," Mr. Gerbati said when he reappeared. "He come soon to take you."

The hair stood up on Jake's head. The man let him eat his breakfast as though nothing was happening and then was going to turn him over to . . . to the goons or the cops or— He got up and fetched his cap and overcoat, though Lord knew he didn't need them, sweating the way he was. Someone rang the bell at the front door.

"Come," Mr. Gerbati ordered. "Is here."

He followed Mr. Gerbati out to the front door. The old man opened it, revealing not a policeman or one of Jake's imagined goons, but Duncan, of all people.

"Hello, Sal," the big man said cheerfully. "Ready to go?" Jake nodded. "You coming, Mr. Gerbati?" Duncan asked.

Mr. Gerbati shook his head. "No. I read my paper."

"Okay. Then it's just us two, Sal."

Jake trailed the big Scot down the stairs. There was a truck standing in the street, the engine *put-putting* as though impatient to be off. "Hop in," Duncan said.

Jake climbed up into the passenger seat. Duncan started down Brook Street and turned left on Main. They were heading toward the town green, toward the city hall, where, Jake knew from his walks around town, there was a police station. He could hardly breathe.

At the green, however, instead of bearing to the right toward the city hall, Duncan bore left up a slight grade. Then he stopped the truck at the tip of a triangular piece of land, well short of the imposing brick building that stood farther up the grade.

"See it?" Duncan asked.

Jake was so relieved that they hadn't parked in front of the city hall that he wasn't even looking straight. "See what? That building up there?"

"No, not the school—the monument . . . there." Now he saw it. In the point of land, as though looking down on all the activities of the town, high on a carved pedestal was a tall granite statue of a man with a coat slung over one arm. "That's our own Bobbie Burns, it is. We Scots paid a pile of money to have that done. Mr. Gerbati wanted you to see it."

What in the blazes was going on? Was Gerbati trying

to tease him? The way a cat toys with a mouse before killing it? And who the devil was Bobbie Burns?

"Get out. You have to look close. It's probably the bonniest granite sculpture in the world." Duncan set the brake and hopped out of the truck. Jake climbed down and accompanied the big Scot over to the statue, which towered over them both. More than three times taller than Duncan himself.

"Every big city puts up its monuments to generals and war heroes, but when it came to the hundredth anniversary of our Bobbie's death, the Scots here wanted the whole town to remember that he was Scotland's greatest poet. The Italians understood. They worship men who write operas. But we couldn't do it ourselves. We mostly get the stone out of the hill. It's the Italians who are the artists. We hired the best that Barclay's shed had to offer. Barclay was one of us Scots, but his carvers were Italian—Novelli and Corti. Novelli carved the great man himself, but look, these panels under the statue—they were Corti's work. Corti was Mr. Gerbati's teacher. Mr. Gerbati followed him here from the old country."

Jake was studying the panels under the statue. There were four scenes, one on each side of the pedestal. Duncan took off his right glove and fingered a panel. "These are from the poems, all but this one—this is his own wee cottage in Ayr. Here—" He took Jake's finger and made it trace the lines of the cottage. "See. You have to feel it. Bas-relief. Harder to do, I think, than a statue." The big Scot shook his head. "God help us. What a waste," he said. "It was just a crazy thing. A fight between the socialists and the anarchists at the Labor Hall, and someone had a gun. Corti wasn't even there for the fight. He was just standing in the wrong place, and some crazy anarchist shoots his pistol off, and *boom!* the greatest carver this side of Italy is dead."

"Do you know . . . ?" How could Jake ask the question? "Do you know why Gerbati wanted you to show me this?"

"*Mr.* Gerbati. I'm not sure. He just called and said he wanted you to see this before you left town. I guess he didn't want you to fail to see the most beautiful thing in the city."

Jake's stomach gave a lurch. "Did he tell you I was leaving?"

"Well, I guess he figures the strike will be over soon and all you kids will be leaving."

"Oh, yeah."

"He wanted to be sure you didn't miss this."

"Why—uh—why didn't he show me himself?"

"He must have thought I could explain it better, being a Scot. Besides, I can always borrow my brother's truck. It's a cold walk from the North End." Duncan grinned and put his glove back on. "Come on, I want to show you one more thing before I take you home." The word "home" sent a spike through Jake's belly, as though the Gerbatis' house could ever be home to the likes of him.

They rode back down Main Street. Duncan didn't even glance toward the city hall. He just drove the noisy, smelly truck along the street, past the shops, taverns, and livery stables. A block before they got to Brook Street, he turned right. They wound up a hill until they stopped at the gates of what was obviously a cemetery. It was here that Duncan pulled over. The road between the gates had not been rolled, much less cleared, so the snow was high. Duncan set the brake. "Can't risk trying to drive in. Can you walk?"

"Yeah," Jake said, though he didn't much like walking into a graveyard, even in broad daylight.

They hiked through snow higher than his new boots, and he could feel it melting on his stockings, but he dared not complain. At last, Duncan stopped. Snow had blown against the stone, and he wiped it off with his large gloved hand. "Here," he said. "Look at this." He was pointing to letters chiseled into the light gray granite. He didn't know that the letters meant nothing to Jake, whose eye was caught by the stream of flowers cascading down the stone. Roses, lilies, daisies, daffodils—all alive in a way that made him sure that Mr. Gerbati had carved them.

"It's his masterpiece," Duncan said. "The boy was his life. First his master dies, then, within the month, his

son. They tell me his hair turned white overnight."
Duncan took off his glove and reverently fingered a rose.
"In the more than eight years since, the man has carved
nothing but flowers, only flowers. It's as though he's
determined to bring dead stone to life."

So this was where Vittorio Gerbati lay—the boy
whose clothes he had put on that first morning. Now
here he was, dead and under the ground, and his father
had made these flowers, which would never die, for him.

"I wanted to show you this, too, before you left. Mr.
Gerbati probably wouldn't have."

They walked in silence to the truck, which was still
put-putting bravely in the cold, and drove back to Brook
Street. Duncan stopped in front of the house. "I won't be
going in," he said. "Can't risk this old crate dying on me.
Been tempting fate all day. See you tomorrow."

"Thanks," said Jake.

"My pleasure, lad."

He opened the front door. Someone was in the parlor—not the sitting room, but the parlor across the hall.
He was talking.

"Come in, Salvatore," Mrs. Gerbati called out as he
tried to pass the door unnoticed. He took off his cap and
went into the room. Mr. Broggi was seated on the best
chair, Mr. and Mrs. Gerbati were on the settee, and Rosa
was on the footstool. "Sit! Sit! Mr. Broggi bring news of
your mamma." Jake perched uneasily on the edge of the

small rocker, not daring to glance at either Rosa or Mr. Gerbati.

"I was just telling your sister here," Mr. Broggi said, "that Mrs. Gurley Flynn—you know?" Jake nodded to indicate that he knew who Mrs. Gurley Flynn was. "She telephone to say Mamma and Anna is okay. They still look to find where baby Ricci is taken, but they will find him soon, sure."

Everyone looked at Jake for some response. "Swell. That's just swell." Rosa glared at him. "Except for the baby," he added hastily.

"Mamma and Anna are still in jail, Sal. Maybe you didn't understand."

"Oh. Oh, yeah. But they'll be out soon, won't they?"

Mr. Broggi beamed. "All the big-city papers is there— Boston, New York, Philadelphia. They tell the whole country about shame of Lawrence, beating up women and little children, snatching babies from mamma's breast, throwing innocent women in jail. Everybody in America'll be mad, be mad as hornets by tomorrow morning. It's great day for the union. My friend, Mr. Savinelli, he call it . . ." He looked around until he had everyone's attention, including Jake's. "He call it 'The Strike for *Pane e Rose.*'"

Rosa started on the stool. "What?" she asked faintly. "*What* do they call it?"

"Bread and Roses. Is beautiful, no? The strikers carry

big sign. It say—" and he used his large stonecutter's hand to shape the words in the air. "It say: 'We want bread and roses, too.'" He beamed. "You understand? Not just bread—hungry, yes. But only bread is not enough. Need roses, too."

Mrs. Gerbati clapped her hands together. "So beautiful!" she said, nodding her head, her eyes closed. "Must be made by Italian."

"It was," Rosa said but so faintly that only Jake, sitting the closest, could hear her.

Mrs. Gerbati herded everyone into the kitchen for cake and coffee. The men laced theirs with some of Mr. Gerbati's grappa. Jake could have used some of it himself, but he didn't dare ask, and none was offered. Rosa picked at her cake, but Jake ate every crumb and took a second slice when Mrs. Gerbati offered.

When Mr. Gerbati returned to the kitchen after seeing Mr. Broggi to the door, he found Mrs. Gerbati at the counter gazing dolefully at her carefully prepared Sunday dinner, which had been left congealing in its own juices since noontime. "He stay so long, my nice food is cold like ice."

"You warm it up," Mr. Gerbati said. "We eat it for supper." He pulled out his watch. "Is nearly time."

She began to protest. "But you have no *dinner!*"

"Is okay, Mrs. Gerbati. No one here starve today."

"We just had cake," Rosa said. "We'll be fine."

Mrs. Gerbati sighed. "I don't like no one go hungry in my house. Everyone eat extra big supper, okay? Now go, go quick, so Rosa and me can fix everything before your poor bellies start to cry," she said, shooing her husband and Jake out of the kitchen.

Mr. Gerbati went toward his chair but didn't sit down. "You have good trip?"

He must mean with Duncan. "Oh, yeah, swell."

"You see Mr. Bobbie Burns?"

"Yeah. Yessir."

"You see Mr. Corti's work?"

"It's very good."

"Good? Is *meraviglioso!* Magnificent!" Mr. Gerbati went back and carefully shut the kitchen door. "Sit, Salvatore."

Now it was coming. The time with Duncan had been a tease after all. But he sat as he had been told to. Mr. Gerbati sat down in his usual chair, took his pipe from his pocket, stuffed it with tobacco, and studied the bowl while he made several attempts to light the contents. Finally, satisfied, he took three or four puffs.

Jake, watching the extended scene, was turning to stone on the nearby chair. *Hell's bells,* why didn't the man get on with it?

"You like Mr. Duncan, no?"

"Yeah, sure. Everyone does."

"He Scot." Mr. Gerbati took another puff. "Like you, maybe?"

"*What?*"

Mr. Gerbati leaned forward. "You no Salvatore Serutti. You no Italian. I don't know who you are—I don't know how come you in my house, in my shed."

What was Jake supposed to say? He opened his mouth, hoping maybe that something would come out of it that made sense to the man, but nothing did.

"Don't trouble make lie to me. Tell me why you come. You know I don't want no boy, but I let you come, yes? Mrs. Gerbati, isn't she good to you? Don't she feed you like her own child?"

Jake studied the toes of his new boots. Already they were scuffed.

"And today. We try to give you what you need— food, warm clothes—but not enough for you, no?" He shook his head. The hair was thick and white like the snow on his son's grave. "I don't know who you are," he said sorrowfully. "I don't know." He put his pipe back into his mouth and studied the smoke curling above it.

"I didn't mean to come." Jake's voice was so small and unlike itself that he almost didn't recognize it. "I'll leave whenever you say. Only please . . ."

Mr. Gerbati took out his pipe and leaned forward, listening.

"Please don't call the police."

"What business I got with police? I live in North End. I don't know what you mean. Who do I call? The priest? The mayor?" He sat back. "I don't even call Mrs. Gerbati. I talk to you. I say, Who are you, boy? Why you lie and make little Rosa lie for you, huh? Is not good, making nice girl like Rosa speak for you, lie for you. Where your shame, boy?"

"I need money."

"So you break my safe? You steal from me and my men? Why don't you ask me, like a man?"

Jake kept his eyes on his boots, his voice hardly above a whisper. "I was scared."

"*Dio mio*. Is that excuse?"

"No, sir."

"Why you need money so bad?" His voice was suddenly gentle.

"I have to buy a train ticket."

"To go home? We buy all the children ticket."

"I can't go back to Lawrence." And then, quite unexpectedly, he realized he was crying. He tried to hide it, but the sobs were shaking his whole body and he couldn't stop. Perhaps it was the relief that Mr. Gerbati wasn't going to call the police or the goons or anyone else. Perhaps it was the hard little man's surprising kindness—like his flowers blooming from the cold gray granite.

The kitchen door opened. Mr. Gerbati shook his head at his wife, and she closed it quickly.

"Go wash your face. Is nearly time to eat. You know Mrs. Gerbati don't like food get cold two time." He got up and knocked his pipe out in the big dish on the table beside his chair. "Later, you tell me. We see what to do, okay?"

Jake sniffed and nodded and hurried to wash up before either Rosa or Mrs. Gerbati could see that he'd been crying.

All through supper, Mrs. Gerbati apologized over the missed *colazione*. She didn't count the cake and coffee they'd shared with Mr. Broggi, or seem to remember that breakfast had been late and more than bountiful. "I promise to feed you childrens three good meal every day, and today only two. Eat, eat," she urged Rosa, who was picking at her food.

"I'm sorry. I just can't stop thinking about—"

"They be fine, Rosa. It don't help Mamma if you don't eat. See, Sal eat good. Make Mamma happy to see how good he eat."

The food tasted, if possible, better than ever to Jake. Mr. Gerbati wasn't going to call the police or anyone else on him. He sneaked a look in the old man's direction. The white head was bowed over his plate. Looking at him, you'd think he didn't even remember what had happened that morning. But he hadn't forgotten. When the meal was over, he quietly asked Jake to come with him to the parlor. "Now we finish our talk," he said.

Mr. Gerbati sat on the settee and waved Jake toward the rocker, but he chose the stool instead.

"Okay," said Mr. Gerbati. "Now we know you no Salvatore Serutti."

"No, sir."

"Tell me, then, who are you?"

"Jake Beale."

"What kind of name is that? Scotch? French? Irish? What?"

"I dunno. Just my name."

"Where is your papa?"

"Dead."

"That is true? No lie?"

"It's true."

"No mamma, neither?"

Jake shook his head. How much did he have to tell the man? Why was it any of his business anyhow?

"So why you sneak and hide, eh? Make little girl take care for you?"

The way he said it made Jake both angry and, if he'd been more familiar with the feeling, ashamed.

"I told you, I was scared."

"Why you scared, boy? You do wrong?"

He nodded. He had done wrong. And before he

could stop himself, the whole story poured out—getting the card from Mrs. Serutti to take home for Pa to sign, finding Pa in bed, waking up to discover that all night long, and for how much longer he did not know, Pa had been dead. The horror of it made him stop in the middle of the telling.

"So you run away?"

"Yessir."

"You was afraid of own poor dead papa?"

He didn't want to say so; it seemed suddenly so cowardly. "Well, I was scared someone—the police, maybe—would find him and blame me."

"Why they blame you? Is freezing cold. He drink too much. It happen, yes? Not your doing."

"I bought him the whiskey."

"Ahh." Mr. Gerbati leaned back against the settee to ponder this. "So then you run and sneak onto train. . . ."

"I thought it was going to New York City. Rosa said she was going to New York."

"New York City is better for you?"

"I could get a job. Take care of myself." Jake studied his hands. They were chapped and the nails were black crescents. "I didn't mean to be trouble for her. As soon as we got to New York, I was going to make a run for it."

The man sat forward again. "Why you always run, boy?"

"I just told you."

"No, I don't think so. I think you run away from *la morte*—from death." He pronounced it "det," which made it sound harsher. Jake wanted to argue but realized he could not.

"So . . . you leave your papa there. Who will bury him? Who will make a stone over his grave?"

"I ain't got the money to do that," Jake mumbled. "Even if I was there, I couldn't do nothing for him."

Mr. Gerbati leaned back again. He patted his pocket, looking for his pipe, but it wasn't there. "So," he said. "We make *uno patto,* what you say, bargain? You and me, we make bargain. You no lie to me no more. You got something to say, you say to me, not send Rosa, okay? You do this, I write union in Lawrence. Tell them to bury your papa. Is not good he not buried yet. Then in spring, I make stone for Papa, okay?"

"Why would you do that?"

"I don't like no man go to grave forgot." He stood up. "We no tell Mrs. Gerbati. Wait for strike to be over, yes? For now, you still her Salvatore."

🌷 Twenty-four

Home at Last

THE BREAD AND ROSES STRIKE! Pride ran like a scarlet ribbon through the anxiety of Rosa's days. People had not only taken notice of their "best sign," some, like Mr. Savinelli, had chosen it as the name of the strike itself. *Their sign*—hers and Mamma's. The one that she had made on their own kitchen table. And Mrs. Gerbati was right; it was Italian to want beauty almost as much as food.

Rosa was painting a new picture of Mamma and Anna in her head. They were in jail, but Mamma was singing, and all the women and girls and children were singing with her. The guards were amazed and then ashamed as they heard the lovely music coming from the throats of the very people they had despised and abused.

She wandered about in a kind of fog. *"We shall not be, we shall not be moved. . . ."* Mamma was singing and everyone else would echo:

"We shall not be, we shall not be moved.
Like a tree planted by the water,
We shall not be moved."

That was Mamma—a beautiful tree. She had been green and lush in the spring of Rosa's childhood, when Papa was alive and there was food and fuel, but even in this, the cruelest of winters, she still stood, her strong branches bare, like silver against the snow and wind. She would bend, but she would not break.

There was no more news for two long days, but Rosa was dry-eyed and somehow less afraid than she had been since before the strike began. When she was able, finally, to turn her attention outside herself, she realized that something was going on with Sal. He was too quiet. He ate—he always ate as though he was scared the food before him might suddenly be snatched away—but he kept his eyes on his bowl or his dinner plate. He didn't slurp his soup as noisily or chew with his mouth so wide open. It was as though he was willing himself to seem smaller, less noticeable. When Mrs. Gerbati ladled more *zuppa* into his bowl or piled more pasta on his plate, he'd glance up quickly and murmur, *"Grazie."*

Mr. Gerbati was quiet, also, but that was not strange. He rarely spoke during a meal. But now his quietness was different, not the closed-in feel of a man keeping everything so tightly under control that he didn't dare open his mouth. No, his whole body seemed looser, more at ease.

Mrs. Gerbati noticed something, too. Rosa could tell, catching the woman watching each of them carefully, giving her husband a smile for no reason. Once, while standing to fill his coffee cup, she rested her free hand lightly on his shoulder. He looked up at her and his eyes were as gentle as Mamma's when she was singing Ricci to sleep. . . . Ah, Ricci, where was he now? Was he somewhere lonely and afraid?

Saturday had been the worst day of her life. Worse than the day Annie Lopizzo had died. Yet here she was, scarcely four days afterward, feeling better. Nothing had changed. There had been no more news, and then she realized what it was. *We shall not be moved.* She had never been able to believe it before.

That very evening, Mr. Gerbati came home from his trip to the shop around the corner, his arms full of newspapers. He marched into the kitchen and, without even taking off his overcoat, spread the papers out on the kitchen table.

"Shoo! Shoo!" Mrs. Gerbati ordered. "Pick up this papers! Where I put my food?"

"Later we eat." Mr. Gerbati said. "Come, Rosa, you read. Is English." He handed her *The New York Herald.*

In a sweep she took in the headlines, and her voice was shaking as she began to read:

BAR SHIPMENT OF STRIKE CHILDREN; WOMEN CLUBBED

Youngsters Trampled in Riot When Lawrence Police Halt Exportation

MOTHERS FIGHT WITH TEETH AND HATPINS

Authorities Descend on Station Where One Hundred Little Ones Were to Entrain for Philadelphia

Rosa looked up, unable to read further. "Hatpins?" she said faintly. Mrs. Marino, perhaps, but never Mamma.

"Mamma and Anna is all right, Rosa," Mrs. Gerbati said. "We hear, remember?"

Rosa nodded. Even so, reading the rest of the article to the eager Mr. Gerbati was not easy. Pictures of Mamma and Anna and maybe even little Ricci being beaten and trampled flooded her mind.

"You see? You see?" Mr. Gerbati cried. "Whole world angry for your mamma now!" He was right of course—every word in the article railed against the brutality of the Lawrence police and the Massachusetts militia. Her voice still shaking, she went on to the next paper. *The Boston Common* was equally incensed. "Police, acting under the orders of the city marshal, clubbed, choked and knocked down women and children, the innocent wives and babies of the strikers. . . ." Rosa stopped midsentence. *Choked?*

"Don't worry, your mamma be okay. Mrs. Gurley Flynn say so," Mr. Gerbati said.

Mrs. Gerbati was stroking Rosa's head, but her hand was trembling. "Knocka down babies," she said. "Who can believe such peoples?"

"Is over," Mr. Gerbati said. "Your mamma win. Now whole world is on her side."

Despite Rosa's renewed anxiety, Mr. Gerbati seemed to be right. Every day brought more news. The whole world *had* turned against Mr. Billy Wood and his fellow mill owners. Congressmen were calling for hearings. Children who worked in the mills were going to Washington to testify. Even the president, Mr. William Howard Taft himself, was asking for investigations into conditions in American industries. And by week's end there was another letter from Anna, this one posted with a real stamp. It read:

Dear Rosa,
You have heard about the truble
at the railway stashun I think. Do

not worry. Mamma and I are fine. I got a bruz on my arm and Mamma got a bump on her head, but we are ok. We are home from jail. The polees took Ricci to the Poor Farm. We did not no where he was, but he is home now and ok to. Mamma says she is sory to giv you so much wory.

The strike is big and better than befor. Mamma says it is wirth a bump on her head and three nites in jail for shure. WE ARE GOING TO WIN. Soon you can come home. We all mis you. Grany J. says the bed is to cold.

Your loving sister Anna,
Mamma and Ricci to

She folded the letter very carefully and returned it to its envelope before she let herself burst into tears.

He supposed he had to tell Rosa, but it included so much lying and hiding the truth that he put it off. She was too worried about her family. She didn't need to hear all his woes—but she would have to, sooner or later. He would wait, he decided, until the strike was truly over. She would be so happy at the thought of going home that she wouldn't waste her time being mad at him and all he'd put her through.

He was still puzzling over his talk with Mr. Gerbati Sunday night. The man had caught him, as they say, red-handed, trying to break into his safe. He hadn't called the police. He hadn't called any of his Italian pals. He had called Duncan. *Because he thought I was Scotch. Even then I was sure he would send me back to Lawrence the next day. But, no, he takes me into his parlor and talks to me. He makes a bargain with me, just like I'm somebody.* But the bargain was that he would stop lying, and if he hadn't told all that many lies to Rosa, he had certainly never told her the truth.

At work he was a demon of energy, racing to the blacksmith shop with points to be sharpened and racing back again, shoveling grout until his shoulders groaned, clearing fresh snow from the path to the door—indeed, doing every job Mr. Gerbati gave him with such speed and devotion that he hardly recognized himself. Now there were only two things left to do. The first was to tell Rosa everything. That should be easy, but he kept putting it off. Then there was the other matter. This, too, he put off, because it meant a kind of begging he'd never let himself stoop to before. Oh, sure, he had begged Mr. Gerbati not to call the police, but he did that out of sheer terror, without any thought. He had turned this new request over in his mind so many times, he had almost worn it out. How could he put it into words? He had tried a thousand times and no words seemed good enough.

The strike would soon be over. Everyone said so. And when the strike was over, the Lawrence children would be sent home. He had to speak to Mr. Gerbati right away. But how?

Barre's entire North End followed the developments in Lawrence as closely as though they'd been mill workers themselves. They still held benefits in the Labor Hall and the opera house, sending the money to the Wobblies in Lawrence. They read almost breathlessly the accounts in the newspapers of the testimony in Washington. The president's own wife, Mrs. William Howard Taft, had gone to hear children from Lawrence talk about their lives in the mills—how they had to sweep the mill floors after working hours for no pay, how money was taken from their meager wages for the water they drank, how little Camella Teoli's hair got caught in the machine and she was scalped.

On Tuesday, March the twelfth, the long-awaited telegram came from Lawrence. Mr. Billy Wood had surrendered. He would meet the strikers' demands—every single one of them. The rest of the mill owners fell like tiles in a game of dominoes. And on Thursday, the fourteenth of March, in the year of our Lord 1912, twenty-five thousand men, women, and children mill workers gathered on Lawrence common and voted to return to work.

The time had come for the Lawrence children to go home. The Barre newspaper on Saturday the sixteenth asked all the families who were hosting children to meet at the Labor Hall the next day, between 10 A.M. and 1 P.M., to make arrangements for the visitors' return. When Mrs. Gerbati and Rosa got home from Mass, Mrs. Gerbati served, with many apologies, an abbreviated breakfast, and then she and Mr. Gerbati headed for the Labor Hall.

Jake and Rosa were left at the house. The committee thought it would be easier for the adults to sort out the details without the children present. "You study now, Salvatore," Mrs. Gerbati said. "Is good chance. Then you go home and show off to Mamma, yes?"

They sat side by side at the kitchen table. Jake hadn't made much progress. He knew his alphabet at least. But Rosa would sigh over the clumsy way he made his letters. He often made the *S*s backward and there were two of them, large capital ones, in Salvatore Serutti. He threw down his pencil.

"It ain't my name, anyway," he said. "I don't need to write it proper."

Rosa cocked her head. "Then tell me your real name. I'll teach you to write that. No need to show it to the Gerbatis."

"Jake," he said. "Jake Beale."

"Hmmph," she said. "I wonder if it has a silent *e*. Beale, that is."

After that, it was easier to tell her the story he had told Mr. Gerbati three weeks earlier. He even told her about robbing the poor box and stealing food and sleeping in the churches, Rosa being as close to a priest as he was ever likely to confess to. He didn't bother to tell her about the trash piles. She knew about those.

"You were running because you thought the police were after you?"

"Yeah. He was dead. I thought they'd blame me." Then he remembered Mr. Gerbati's admonition. "Not just that. I reckon I was spooked. I'd slept all night with a corpse. It really spooked me."

She nodded. "It would scare me, too," she said and shuddered. It made him feel better, Rosa saying that.

As little as he wanted to, he made himself tell Rosa the events of that awful Sunday when he'd tried to break into Mr. Gerbati's safe. Her hand flew to her mouth, and her whole face went white.

"I know," he said. "I done a terrible wrong. I don't know why he didn't drag me to the police the minute he caught me. He didn't beat me or nothing. He just made me promise to stop lying. And I'm trying."

It took him a minute to realize that Rosa was crying.

"C'mon, Rosa. What's the matter? I told you I was trying."

"It's not that." She looked up at him, her face streaked with tears. "It's my prayers," she said. "They've all been answered. The strike is over. Mamma and Anna and Ricci are safe. I'm going home soon. And you confessed your sins. The Virgin answered my prayers and"— here she burst into fresh tears—"and I'm not even good."

"Sure, you're good. You're the best person I know."

"No, I'm not. And all my prayers were answered anyway—well, all except for one."

"What one was that?"

"I prayed you could be as happy as me."

When the Gerbatis came in sometime later, Mrs. Gerbati went straight to the kitchen. The noon meal would be very late and, by her standards, breakfast had been nothing. Food took precedence over delivering news, apparently. The meal was on the table—soup to cake—before Mr. Gerbati cleared his throat, took a noisy gulp of his grappa-laced coffee, and began.

"Okay," he said. "We talk and make plan today. Thirty-five children come, two go back right away, yes?" Everyone agreed. "Then week before this there was four children go home because someone in family very sick, yes?" They all remembered, especially Rosa, who had not really wished illness upon any member of her family, but still. . . . "Then yesterday, one more." Rosa hadn't heard about that one. "That leave," he signaled with his fingers, "twenty-eight children, yes?" They all nodded. "Tomorrow Mr. Broggi can take some children, but twenty-eight too many, so some have to wait."

Rosa clamped her hand over her mouth. Otherwise, she was sure to cry out. How could she wait any longer? Mrs. Gerbati reached over and gently took the hand away. "I tell them my Rosa need to go," she said. "I don't want to lose my childrens, but they need their own mamma, yes?"

"You've been so good to us, Mrs. Gerbati. We do thank you both, but . . ."

Jake stiffened. Maybe he'd left talking to Mr. Gerbati until it was too late. It sounded as though they were going to be shipped back to Lawrence tomorrow. *Hell's bells,* why had he put it off?

"So," said Mr. Gerbati, "Rosa need to be ready for train tomorrow in afternoon. Mamma already know. She will meet you."

"Oh," Rosa said, suddenly remembering him. "What about Salvatore? When does he leave?"

Mr. Gerbati swung around and looked Jake in the eye. "Is very strange thing. On the list come from Lawrence union committee, isn't no Salvatore Serutti."

"Don't worry, Salvatore," Mrs. Gerbati said. "We straighten. You be home soon. *Ti prometto.* Is a promise."

Monday morning Jake and Mr. Gerbati went to work as usual. All the way there, Jake tried to make himself talk to the man, but Mr. Gerbati walked so fast and was so intent on getting to the shed that Jake's courage failed him once again.

Meanwhile, at the house, Rosa climbed the stairs to her beautiful bedroom for the last time. She was looking about, determined to keep the picture of it in her mind forever, when she heard Mrs. Gerbati's heavy step on the stairs.

"*Scusami,* Rosa." She stood panting at the door, a leather suitcase in one hand, her other arm full of clothing. "I send few things to home."

"Oh, Mrs. Gerbati . . ." She didn't know what to say.

"No, no, is nothing." Mrs. Gerbati came into the room and dumped her load onto the bed. "And bag for train." She began to fold the garments and put them into the case.

Rosa stared wide-eyed, then slowly began to help. More underwear, another dress—"For your Anna"—a set of small boy's underwear, trousers, shirt, and jacket—"For little Ricci. I don't know size so I get big, okay?"—two woolen shawls—"One for Anna and one for Mamma, eh?"

Tears were falling on everything Rosa folded. "No, no! Don't cry! Then I cry. No good we cry. Is happy time, yes?" The woman put her arms around Rosa, and Rosa could feel the old body shake with sobs. Mrs. Gerbati pulled away and wiped her eyes on her apron. "Silly old woman, eh?"

"No," said Rosa and turned to hide fresh tears. "You're too kind, Mrs. Gerbati, but not silly. Never silly." She busied herself getting the extra underwear and clothes Mrs. Gerbati had bought for her out of the bureau to add to the wealth already packed.

In the end, Mrs. Gerbati had to sit on the case before Rosa could close it. They were both laughing by the time Rosa managed to pull her to her feet again.

Mrs. Gerbati laid out even more than her usual noon-day feast. No one talked much. Rosa toyed with her food. As the time for departure grew closer, it became harder to hide her excitement. She was going home at last.

"You don't eat, Rosa? Long ride to Lawrence," Mr. Gerbati said.

Rosa shook her head. "It's good, really it is, I just can't . . ."

"Our Rosa is happy girl today," Mrs. Gerbati said. "But we miss her, don't we, Mr. Gerbati, Salvatore?"

"I'll miss you, too," Rosa said.

Jake looked at her closely, as though to make sure she wasn't lying.

"I wish Sal was coming with me," she said.

"Oh, it work out for Salvatore," Mr. Gerbati said. "I talk to committee. Everything fixed." He glanced across the table at Mrs. Gerbati, and then focused on his coffee.

⚜   ⚜   ⚜

The three of them went to see Rosa off on the train even though it meant that Jake and Mr. Gerbati would be late getting back to work. The other host families of the returning children were there, chattering and hugging and promising to keep in touch.

"You write letter, Rosa, yes?" Mrs. Gerbati said. "Tell about Mamma and Anna and little Ricci, okay?"

"Of course I will," Rosa said. "And I'll write to Sal, too."

"Good practice for Salvatore," Mrs. Gerbati said. "Learn to read good, eh?"

Jake looked at his boots.

"You've got to practice, you know," Rosa said. "Promise me you'll work on it."

"Yeah, okay," he said, but he didn't look up. Why were they talking about reading when the train whistle was already blowing? She was going, and what would happen to him now? He watched the train chug slowly into the station.

Rosa hugged each of the Gerbatis. Then she turned to him. He thought for a moment she was going to hug him, too, but, instead, she put out her hand and, a bit shyly, took his. "Goodbye for now, Sal . . . Jake," she whispered. "You behave, hear?"

He nodded, his throat a bit too full to get out words. Then, quickly, she was on the train, waving from the window.

The three of them stood there in a little huddle, Mrs. Gerbati wiping her tears away with the tail of her shawl.

So long, shoe girl. Thanks for everything. He lifted his hand and began to wave until he could no longer see the southbound train, its whistle scarcely a tiny peep piercing the March fog.

"Mrs. Gerbati," Mr. Gerbati said sternly. "How come you don't buy this boy no gloves? Look how red his hands is."

"Oh," said Mrs. Gerbati. "I do today. Now, before he go back to work."

"Don't you mind," Mr. Gerbati said. "I do already." Out of his big overcoat pocket he pulled a pair of brown leather gloves. "So, try on. See if they fit good."

The gloves were soft and lined with fleece. Jake pulled them on slowly. *Would the man never cease to surprise?*

"So, fit okay?"

"Perfect."

"Oh," said Mrs. Gerbati, shaking her head. "No good, Mr. Gerbati. Should buy big. He grow too fast."

"So," Mr. Gerbati said, "next year we buy him new pair."

Next year? Jake looked at Mr. Gerbati. The old man shrugged. Mrs. Gerbati was smiling across her wide face, fresh tears swimming in her dark eyes. She threw her arms around Jake and crushed him to her breast. "We need boy in our house," she said in his ear.

It was a hug to smother a small army of boys, but Jake didn't even care. He was never going to have to beg to stay. *Hell's bells.* He wasn't even going to have to ask. They had straightened it out, just as Mrs. Gerbati had promised. He stepped away from her to wipe his nose on the back of his sleeve, careful to avoid his beautiful new gloves.

"I guess it's time we was getting back to work, eh, Mr. Gerbati?"

The old man pulled out his watch. *"Si,"* he said. "Longa past time. You run ahead, Salva—Mr. Jake Beale. Tell those men I'm on the way."

And Jake Beale began to run. Even though his new boots sometimes slipped on the icy cobbles, he did not stumble. How strange, how wonderful it seemed to be running, not away from petty crime or deadly fear, but toward a new life where bread was never wanting and roses grew in stone.

❧ Historical Note

At the turn of the twentieth century, the industrial revolution in the United States was at its height. But in order to keep profits high, owners needed increased numbers of laborers who would work for low wages. The owners of the enormous textile mills in Lawrence, Massachusetts, sent agents to poverty-stricken areas of Europe to recruit whole families to come to their mills. Posters were displayed showing an immigrant man leaving a Lawrence factory carrying a bag of gold, heading toward a bank across the street. By 1912, there were workers in Lawrence from at least thirty different countries speaking forty-five languages. The earliest workers had been mostly native-born or Irish. The Irish quickly rose to positions of importance, not only in the mills but in the city itself. In 1881, John Breen, an Irish Catholic undertaker, was elected mayor. The John Breen involved in the abortive dynamite plot was his son.

Conditions in the mills were very difficult for the

new immigrant workers. They usually had the lowest-paying jobs. In order for families to survive, everyone who was able had to go to work. If children were under the age of fourteen, parents often paid to have their birth certificates falsified so the children could work in the mill.

In 1911, the Massachusetts state legislature ordered mill owners to cut the working hours of women and children from fifty-six a week to fifty-four, beginning January 1, 1912. Since most men made higher wages than women, the mill owners cut everyone's hours to fifty-four, speeded up the machines, and cut pay to make up for any lost profits that might result from the shortened work week.

The Italian branch of the Industrial Workers of the World (IWW), led by Angelo Rocco, a twenty-five-year-old worker who went to high school at night, determined to strike if pay was cut. Rocco felt the workers, coming from so many countries and speaking so many languages, would need help if they were to organize an effective strike. He telegraphed Joseph Ettor, one of the IWW's professional organizers, and asked him to come to Lawrence. Ettor, who was Italian American, was a charismatic speaker in several languages. He arrived in the city soon after the massive walkout on January 12 and immediately established a local strike committee, which included a woman, Mrs. Annie Welzenbach, and represented a number of nationalities. Ettor also organized relief efforts for the strikers and their families, who had been living on the edge of starvation even when working full-time.

Aided by the organizing efforts of Ettor and his compatriot, the Italian poet Arturo Giovannitti, and then, after their imprisonment on false charges, by Big Bill Haywood and Elizabeth Gurley Flynn, the strikers, especially the immigrant women, maintained an amazing solidarity throughout the two months of the strike. "The women won the strike," Haywood was quoted as saying.

Others said it was the songs that brought the strikers to victory. Little red books containing union songs were passed out. Although most of the women couldn't read English, somehow they learned to sing in a way that made the police and militia tremble. "Beware that movement," one observing journalist said, "that generates its own songs."

On September 28, 1912, Ettor, Giovannitti, and a local worker, Joseph Caruso, were put on trial for the murder of Annie Lopizzo. Crowds stood outside the courtroom, declaring that the strike would not be truly ended until these men were set free.

The trial dragged on until November 23, when Ettor, Giovannitti, and Caruso were found not guilty. On Thanksgiving Day thousands gathered to cheer them. Those cheers reverberated through the Socialist Labor

Hall of Barre, Vermont, and in union halls across the country.

The city of Barre was also very much an immigrant city. The area was long known for its high-quality granite, but granite could not be profitably quarried until the advent of modern derricks and steam drills, and it could not be widely sold until 1888, when a railroad line was built to reach the hill quarries. Then, all at once, a large supply of labor was needed. Aberdeen, Scotland, was going through severe economic times, and the quarries there were shut down, so many Scottish quarriers immigrated to Barre. They were followed by Scandinavian, Spanish, English, Greek, Swiss, Austrian, and French Canadian workers, and, of course, the Italian sculptors who left the marble industry in northern Italy to carve Barre granite. Sadly, in the early 1900s, work in the granite sheds of Vermont, where windows were shuttered against the cold weather, caused many of them to die young of silicosis, a story told in the novel *Like Lesser Gods* by Mari Tomasi. Modern ventilating equipment has virtually eliminated this threat to the health of stonecutters, and the last recorded death from silicosis occurred in 1932.

The early Italian immigrants were very active politically, many of them having been socialists or anarchists in Italy. They lived in tight-knit families, mostly in the North End of the city, and were in the early years regarded with some prejudice by native Vermonters. The granite industry in Barre still flourishes, although only a fraction of the labor force of 1912 is at work in the industry today. The old Socialist Labor Hall has been restored and is the site of many community events. Barre's sculptors are still highly regarded. One, Frank Gaylord, was the creator of the Korean War Memorial in Washington, D.C., and although the granite for the Vietnam Veterans Memorial is not Barre gray, the black granite of the memorial was brought to Barre to be engraved and polished.

The people of Barre remember with pride the fact that they were able to help the mill workers of Lawrence during the 1912 strike. Not only did the Italian stonecutters take in children of strikers, they also raised hundreds of dollars for strike relief. After Ettor and Giovannitti were freed, Giovannitti came to Barre for ten days and spoke in the Labor Hall, where, according to *The Barre Daily Times,* he "avoided the subject of politics and stated his simple desire to let his audience know just how much their support had meant to the textile operatives."

There is considerable debate about the term "Bread and Roses;" as applied to the 1912 strike. Folklore has it that there was a photograph of marchers taken during the strike that showed a placard reading, variously, "We want bread and roses, too" or "Give us bread, Give us roses" or "We want bread and we want roses, too." The actual photograph has never surfaced. Whether the Italian slogan *"Pane e Rose,"* was used by the Italian strikers in Lawrence is, at best, unsure. Nor do we know the date when Giovanitti wrote the Italian poem *"Pan' e Rose."* The English poem "Bread and Roses" was not inspired by the strike, according to its author, James Oppenheim, but as it was set to music not long afterward, the song has generally been associated with the Lawrence strike. By making Mamma and Rosa responsible for the legendary slogan and making it part of this story, I have obviously placed the incident in the realm of fiction rather than verifiable fact.

🐾 Acknowledgments

I am particularly indebted to Dr. Richard F. Ciccarelli of Lawrence, Massachusetts, and Karen Lane of Barre, Vermont, for reading the manuscript and making helpful suggestions and corrections, though any errors that remain are my own. Dr. Ciccarelli's father, like many young mill workers, was the son of Italian immigrants. He went to work with falsified papers at the age of eleven, got his education in night school extension courses, and became a pharmacist. Ms. Lane is the director of the Aldrich Public Library in Barre and cheerfully gathered together many sources for me. A student of Barre history, she has been instrumental in the restoration of the Socialist Labor Hall in Barre that appears in the novel and is now designated by the National Park Service as a National Historic Landmark. She also introduced me to Giuliano Cecchinelli, who came as a seventeen-year-old from Carrara, Italy, to the marble works in Proctor, Vermont, and migrated north to Barre to carve granite. Mr. Cecchinelli has been called the "last of the Italians," and, indeed, as he showed Karen and me around the granite shed where he is the chief sculptor, I felt as though he could have stepped out of the pages of this book.

I would also like to thank Russell Belding who is laboriously assembling every mention of the Socialist Labor Hall from *The Barre Daily Times, The Montpelier Evening Argus,* and other periodicals of the era, and whose knowledge of Main Street and the Barre city schools during this period I drew upon. Thanks, too, to Jim Beauchesne at the Lawrence Heritage State Park, who pointed me toward many helpful sources, including the rousing documentary film "Collective Voices: The Bread and Roses Strike" and a number of helpful booklets published by the Immigrant City Archives in Lawrence. Also, thanks are due to David Malone for tracking down facts about Italian immigration to Lawrence and to Jim Armstrong for his careful copyediting of the manuscript.

Among the books that I depended on are: Donald B. Cole, *Immigrant City: Lawrence, Massachusetts, 1845–1921* (Chapel Hill: University of North Carolina Press, 1991); Ardis Cameron, *Radicals of the Worst Sort: Laboring Women in Lawrence, Massachusetts, 1860–1912* (Urbana: University of Illinois Press, 1995); William Moran, *The Belles of New England: The Women of the Textile Mills and the Families Whose Wealth They Wove* (New York: Thomas

Dunne Books, St. Martin's Press, 2002); *Rebel Voices: An IWW Anthology*, edited, with introductions, by Joyce L. Kornbluh (Chicago: Charles W. Kerr Publishing Company, 1998); William Cahn, *Lawrence 1912: The Bread and Roses Strike* (New York: The Pilgrim Press, 1977); Dorothy and Thomas Hoobler, *The Italian American Family Album* (New York: Oxford University Press, 1994); Fred E. Beal, *Proletarian Journey: New England, Gastonia, Moscow* (New York: Da Capo Press, 1971); Elizabeth Gurley Flynn, *The Rebel Girl: An Autobiography* (New York: International Publishers, 1973); Mari Tomasi, *Like Lesser Gods* (Shelburne, Vt.: New England Press, 1988); Mari Tomasi and Roaldus Richmond, writers and interviewers, and Alfred Rosa and Mark Wanner, editors, *Men Against Granite* (Shelburne, Vt.: New England Press, 2004); Rod Clarke, *Carved in Stone: A History of the Barre Granite Industry* (Barre, Vt.: The Rock of Ages Corporation, 1989).

I hope this book honors in part the debt I owe to my editor of thirty-five years, Virginia Buckley, whose parents were Italian immigrants. Her father, in time, earned a Ph.D. and became a professor of romance languages at The City College of New York, and her mother was a Phi Beta Kappa graduate of Hunter College in New York.

And, as always, this book would never have been finished without the support of my longtime and long-suffering husband, John Paterson.